The Graywolf Short Fiction Series

D0121710

1 9 9 1

THE

L O O M

AND OTHER STORIES

R. A. SASAKI

GRAYWOLF PRESS

"The Loom" was included in *Making Waves: An Anthology of Writings by Asian-American Women* (Beacon Press, 1989).

"Wild Mushrooms" was previously published in the *Short Story Review* (Spring 1988).

Publication of this volume is made possible in part by a grant provided by the Minnesota State Arts Board, through an appropriation by the Minnesota State Legislature, and by a grant from the National Endowment for the Arts. Additional support has been provided by the Jerome Foundation, the Northwest Area Foundation, and other generous contributions from foundations, corporations, and individuals. Graywolf Press is a member agency of United Arts, Saint Paul.

Published by Graywolf Press
2402 University Avenue, Suite 203, Saint Paul, Minnesota 55114.
All rights reserved.

ISBN 1-55597-157-1

9 8 7 6 5 4 3 2 1
First Printing, 1991

Library of Congress Cataloging-in-Publication Data

Sasaki, Ruth A., 1952-
  The loom and other stories / R.A. Sasaki.
     p.   cm. — (The Graywolf short fiction series)
  ISBN 1-55597-157-1
    1. Japanese-Americans—Fiction.   I. Title.   II. Series.
PS3569.A745L66   1991   91-15574
813'.54—dc 20

To my mother and father

Contents

"And out of a pattern of lies, art weaves the truth."
— *D. H. Lawrence*

ANOTHER

WRITER'S

BEGINNINGS

I was an ugly child. I had a long horse face, not much of a nose, and two front teeth that got in the way no matter what I tried to do, and made my expressions for surprise, friendliness, confusion, and anger all look the same. On top of that, my hair, lopped straight across the front above the eyebrows and straight around from side to side just above the earlobes, looked like a lumberjack had taken a buzz saw to it. Actually, my father was not a lumberjack. Neither was he a barber; but for some reason, it always fell to him to do the job. As if that weren't enough, I had glasses that winged up like the back fins of a Cadillac — white, speckled with silver.

I was sheltered from the crushing reality of my own plainness by the reassurances of a loving family. I was no different from other little girls in that I spent long hours before my mother's looking glass trying out different expressions, poses, angles, looking for that glimmer of beauty that could make me a Mouseketeer. My sister had a much better sense of reality. She knew, at the age of eight, that there was no such thing as a Japanese Mouseketeer. Reality never stopped *me* from hoping. Had I been aware of it, it might have. But I was oblivious. That was the source of my confidence.

My first inkling of my ugliness was when I brought home my fifth-grade school picture. There I was in a pink dress with a white collar, bangs cut straight across my face, their line marred only by the Cad fins winging up to each corner. It looked like I had a mouth full of marbles. (It was just my teeth.) I dutifully delivered the picture over to my mother, without pride, without apology, in the same way I'd hand over a report card — impersonally, dissociating myself from it so that whatever the reaction, I would not be culpable. Then I retired to the stairway as my mother studied the picture.

There was a rather long silence, followed by a sigh.

You have to know my mother in order to understand just how devastating this reaction was, even in my dissociated state. My mother believes in being positive. One summer when we went to Yosemite, the waterfalls were dry. My sister expressed her disappointment in a postcard to a friend: "There's no water in Yosemite Falls." My mother was horrified. "You shouldn't write a thing like that," she chided. "You should say Yosemite is beautiful and you're having a wonderful time."

Well, when my mother saw my fifth-grade picture, I knew there was no water in Yosemite Falls; but I expected some sort of encouraging remark. I realized the extent of my plainness when even my mother could find absolutely nothing to say. I was sorry for her, and thought she deserved better, a daughter like my friend Marilyn, for example, who was cute and sweet and always took Shirley Temple pictures full of personality. Instead, she had this horse-faced daughter whose picture was full of teeth. Teeth and wings.

So for the first time I considered the possibility that I might not make it as a Mouseketeer after all. Looks would never be my meal ticket. I would have to develop other talents.

OHAKA-MAIRI

The car turns smoothly under my father's hand. Silently, it slips onto the freeway, heading south.

"Too cold back there?" my father asks, glancing at me in the rearview mirror and rolling up his window.

"No." The air is suddenly close.

"Jo hasn't been to see her yet," my mother says. "She should once, before she goes away in the fall."

It has been two years, after all. But why must we go to this long-ago place, this place left behind in windswept memories? Until now, I have grieved for her in my own way, in my own places.

I don't know whether something in the air carried a silent message discernible only to my mother, or whether it was some inner clock at work that only she possessed, but about two or three times a year she would suddenly say to the rest of the family: "Mo, it's about time we went ohaka-mairi." And we would go that weekend.

We would all pile into the car and head south, out of the city. From San Francisco, Sunday drives with the family could take us in any of three directions. Each direction had special significance, emotional coloring. North was a warm, sunny direction. It meant crossing the Golden Gate Bridge. It meant rolling hills and sleepy harbor towns. It almost always meant an ice cream cone. East meant getting up before dawn and going to Yosemite. We did this every summer. South was chilly, south was sad. The fog always made us hunch down in our seats, shivering. South meant either the airport, to say good-bye, or the cemetery.

My father is looking at me in the rearview mirror. My hands tingle, bloodless. I am sitting on them.

I want to remember her as she was the night she brought Jeff home with her. She came through the front door like a fresh wind, fire-cheeked and blooming, hair a hopeless tangle falling to her waist. I laughed, and my fingers became trapped in the knotted black mass as I tried to untangle it. She laughed, and stopped moving just long enough for me to get my fingers out. She was home.

But Jeff was there. He stood between the living room where my father sat and the kitchen where my mother was putting away her apron, looking as though he had brought all of outdoors in with him. But all of outdoors did not fit into our house. Standing in our entryway against black lacquer and flowered scrolls, beard bristling over ruddy skin, boots crusted with the dried earth of another world, he was like a giant redwood among the potted bonsai of my father's house. My mother came hurrying from the kitchen, bowing instinctively. I retreated to the stairway, from which I could see my father sitting in his armchair, perfectly still.

The next time I saw Jeff was after she died.

The cemetery was like a city of tombstones, laid out in neat rows with intersections and streets along which neither cars nor people moved, only dust. It was always windy. We would stop at one of the flower shops along the side of the road, where my father would buy flowers — usually carnations, because they are a hardy flower and last a long time after cut. Then we would turn into the cemetery and park on the dusty road. My mother and father would clip the hedge that grew on my grandparents' plot, pour water over the headstone, rake the dead leaves. My sisters and I would play hide-and-seek among the tombstones. Some of them were big enough to stand behind.

On the day she died, relatives came and went like figures in a dream. I sat alone in the house, watching out the window, hearing the voices of aunts and uncles downstairs stifling the laughter of children and worrying about lunch. The doorbell kept ringing, and I would open the door and stare blankly at whoever stood outside until my aunt came to usher them in.

The coroner's report spoke only of an inanimate object. Date, time, place, injuries sustained, cause of death.

Our car eases into the exit lane. We leave the freeway, and pass a row of drive-ins. A large red and white barrel floats by. My father catches my eye in the rearview mirror. Perhaps he is remembering that last early-morning fishing expedition, when she and I filled a Kentucky Fried Chicken bucket with sand crabs. We went shrieking along the beach after the scuttling crabs, and the only reason I got myself to pick one up was because she did it first. At the end of the day, we left the tracks of our *zori* entwined in the wet sand. The bucket was still full. Let them go, my father had said. We were reluctant. All that work. We vowed to do this again, next weekend if possible. But we didn't.

We met with Jeff two months after the funeral, my sisters and I. It was just lunch, a sandwich eaten outside on the grass. It was the third and last time I saw him, the second being at the banquet after my sister's funeral when my father, in fury mixed up with grief, had ordered him to leave. We had not had a chance to get to know Jeff, and now it seemed too late. He was a stranger. I searched his face, looking for whatever it was that my sister had loved. There were so many questions I wanted to ask, but I thought of the night he had spent trapped, alone on that ledge after she fell, and I could not ask them. We spoke of unimportant things, even made a few jokes. Then we said good-bye. A year later, he went away, to Canada. Now I am leaving, too.

Flower shops begin appearing along the side of the road. We are almost there. We pull into the parking lot of one of the shops. The window is filled with heavy-looking floral displays. I can almost smell them from here. *I remember the odor of carnations, mingled with the scent of incense, at the funerals of the old issei friends of my grandparents in the Buddhist church, when I was a child.*

My father gets out of the car. Through the display window I see him enter the store. I follow his jet-black head, touched with white, as it weaves among the bulbous flowers, turning, stopping, hesitant, as if suddenly lost in the vision of a toddling child with flaming cheeks and bowl-shaped cap of hair.

"I was really crushed when I realized that your parents didn't want to hear what I had to say," Jeff wrote in a letter from Canada. "I wanted us to face the pain together, to tell them about this daughter of theirs, her thoughts and feelings that only I knew. But that has passed. I don't care anymore."

My father stops before a bucket of spring blossoms.

"I don't blame your father for being bitter. But I do condemn him for not admitting that she was a person different from the person he wanted her to be. He will die with bitterness, never having known her. . . . "

When my father comes out of the store, he carries a delicate branch of spring blossoms. He gives them to my mother, and we cross the road. We pull into a circular drive, stop on the dusty road. Everything is still. The engine dies. My father fumbles with the doors as we get out. My parents lead the way, heads bowed, and I want to run, to bolt away from the dusty and inevitable avenue.

But something catches my eye. On the ground at my feet is a single pink petal, flickering in the dust. Another falls, in my father's footsteps.

"You say you want to understand me. There's a book you might read, about the mountains. I'll send you a copy. Your sister loved it too. You might even learn something about her. Love, Jeff"

I start slowly down the avenue of tombstones where we hid as children; I come seeking her again. My father turns the corner and I turn the corner and there is her name, her name.

THE

LOOM

It was when Cathy died that the other Terasaki sisters began to think that something was wrong with their mother. Sharon and Jo were home for the weekend, and when the phone call came they had gone up to her room with the shocking news, barely able to speak through their tears. Sharon had to raise her voice so her mother could hear the awful words, choked out like bits of shattered glass, while Jo watched what seemed like anger pull her mother's face into a solemn frown.

"You see?" their mother said. Her voice, harsh and trembling with a shocking vehemence, startled the two sisters even in their grief. "Daddy told her not to go mountain climbing. He said it was too dangerous. She didn't listen."

Recalling her words later, Jo felt chilled.

They had always known about their mother's "ways" — the way she would snip off their straight black hair when they were children as soon as it grew past their ears, saying that hair too long would give people the wrong idea. Then later, when they were grown and defiant and wore their hair down to their waists, she would continue to campaign by lifting the long strands and snipping at them with her fingers. There was also the way she would tear through the house in a frenzy of cleaning just before they left on a family vacation, "in case there's a fire or someone breaks in and *yoso no hito* have to come in." They never understood if it was the firemen, the police, or the burglar before whose eyes she would be mortally shamed if her house were not spotless. There was even the way she cooked. She was governed not by inspiration or taste, but by what "they" did. The clothes she chose for them were what "they" were wearing these days. Who is this "they"? her daughters always wanted to ask her. Her idiosyncrasies were a source of mild frustration to which the girls were more or less resigned. "Oh, Mom," they would groan, or, to each other: "That's just Mom."

But this.

"It was as though she didn't feel anything at all," Jo recounted to her eldest sister, Linda, who had come home from Germany for the funeral. "It was as though all she could think about was that Cathy had broken the rules."

It wasn't until their father had come home that their mother cried, swept along in the wake of his massive grief. He had been away on a weekend fishing trip, and they had tried to get in touch with him, but failed. Jo had telephoned the highway patrol and park rangers at all his favorite fishing spots, saying, "No, don't tell him that his daughter has died. Would you just tell him to come home as soon as possible?" And it was Jo who was standing at the window watching when his truck turned the corner for home. The three women went down to the basement together. He and his fishing buddy had just emerged from the dusty, fish-odorous truck, and he was rolling up the garage door when they reached him. He was caught between the bright spring sunlight and the dark coolness of the basement. His hand still on the garage door, he heard the news of his daughter's death. Their mother told him, with a hint of fear in her voice. He cried, as children cry who have awakened in the night to a nameless terror, a nameless grief; for a suspended moment, as he stood alone sobbing his dead daughter's name, the three women deferred to the sanctity of his suffering. Then Sharon moved to encircle him in her arms, clinging flimsily to him against the tremendous isolation of grief.

It was only then that their mother had cried, but it

seemed almost vicarious, as if she had needed their father to process the raw stuff of life into personal emotion. Not once since the death had she talked about her own feelings. Not ever, her daughters now realized.

"It would probably do Mom good to get away for a while," Linda said. "I was thinking of taking her to Germany with me when I go back, just for a few weeks. She's never been anywhere. A change of scene might be just what she needs. Don't you think?"

"I suppose it's worth a try," Jo said.

So it was decided that when Linda flew back to join her husband, who was stationed in Heidelberg, their mother would go with her and stay a month. Except for a visit to Japan with her own mother when she was sixteen, it was their mother's first trip abroad. At first she was hesitant, but their father encouraged her; he would go too if he didn't have to stay and run the business.

It was hard to imagine their mother outside the context of their house. She had always been there when the children came back from school; in fact, the sisters had never had babysitters. Now, as they watched her at the airport, so small and sweet with her large purse clutched tightly in both hands and her new suitcase neatly packed and properly tagged beside her, they wondered just who was this little person, this person who was their mother?

She had grown up in San Francisco, wearing the two faces of a second-generation child born of immigrant parents. The two faces never met; there was no common thread running through both worlds. The duality was unplanned, untaught. Perhaps it had begun the first day of school when she couldn't understand the teacher and Eleanor Leland had called her a "Jap" and she cried. Before then there had never been a need to sort out her identity; she had met life headlong and with the confidence of a child.

Her world had been the old Victorian flat in which her mother took in boarders — the long, narrow corridor, the spiral stairway, the quilts covered with bright Japanese cloth, and the smell of fish cooking in the kitchen. She had accepted without question the people who padded in and out of her world on stockinged feet; they all seemed to be friends of the family. She never wondered why most of them were men, and it never occurred to her child's mind to ask why they didn't have their own families. The men often couldn't pay, but they were always grateful. They lounged in doorways and had teasing affectionate words for her and her sister. Then they would disappear, for a month, for six months, a year. Time, to a child, was boundless and unmeasurable. Later, crates of fruit would arrive and be stacked in the corridor. "From Sato-san," her mother would say, or, "*Kudoh-san kara.*"

The young men sometimes came back to visit with new hats set jauntily on their heads, if luck was good. But often luck was not good, and they came back to stay, again and again, each stay longer than the last; and each time they would tease less and drink more with her father in the back room. The slap of cards rose over the low mumble of their longing and despair. All this she accepted as her world.

The Victorian house which contained her world was on Pine Street, and so it was known as "Pine" to the young adventurers from her parents' native Wakayama prefecture in Japan who made their way from the docks of Osaka to the lettuce fields and fruit orchards of California. "Stay at

Pine," the word passed along the grapevine, "Moriwaki-
san will take care of you."

It was a short walk down the Buchanan Street hill from
Pine to the flats where the Japanese community had taken
root and was thriving like a tree whose seed had blown in
from the Pacific and had held fast in this nook, this fold in
the city's many gradations. When she was a little older her
world expanded beyond the Victorian called Pine. It expanded toward the heart of this community, toward the
little shops from which her mother returned each day,
string bag bulging with newspaper-wrapped parcels and a
long white radish or two. She played hide-and-seek among
the barrels of pickles and sacks of rice piled high in the garage that claimed to be the American Fish Market while her
mother exchanged news of the comings and goings of the
community over the fish counter. "Ship coming in Friday?
Do you think Yamashita-san's picture bride will come?
She's in for a surprise!"

At the age of five she roller-skated to the corner of her
block, then on sudden impulse turned the corner and
started down the Buchanan Street hill. Her elder sister,
Keiko, who had expected her to turn around and come
right back, threw down her jump rope and ran after her,
screaming for her to stop. But she didn't stop. She made it
all the way to the bottom, cheeks flushed red and black hair
flying, before shooting off the curb and crumpling in the
street. Her hands and knees were scraped raw, but she was
laughing.

Before that first day of school there had been no need to
look above Pine Street, where the city reached upwards to
the Pacific Heights area and the splendid mansions of the

rich white people. The only Japanese who went to Pacific Heights were the ones employed to do housecleaning as day laborers. She had always known what was on the other side of Pine Street, and accepted easily that it was not part of her world.

When it came time for her to go to school, she was not sent to the same school as the other Japanese-American children because Pine was on the edge of Japantown and in a different school district. She was the only Japanese in her class. And from the instant Eleanor Leland pulled up the corners of her eyes at her, sneering "Jap!", a kind of radar system went to work in her. Afterward she always acted with caution in new surroundings, blending in like a chameleon for survival. There were two things she would never do again: one was to forget the girl's name who had called her a Jap, and the other was to cry.

She did her best to blend in. Though separated from the others by her features and her native tongue, she tried to be as inconspicuous as possible. If she didn't understand what the teacher said, she watched the other children and copied them. She listened carefully to the teacher and didn't do anything that might provoke criticism. If she couldn't be outstanding she at least wanted to be invisible.

She succeeded. She muted her colors and blended in. She was a quiet student and the other children got used to her; some were even nice to her. But she was still not really a part of their world because she was not really herself.

At the end of each school day she went home to the dark, narrow corridors of the old Victorian and the soothing, unconscious jumble of two tongues that was the two generations' compromise for the sake of communication. Theirs was a comfortable language, like a comfortable old sweater that had been well washed and rendered shapeless by wear. She would never wear it outside of the house. It was a personal thing, like a hole in one's sock, which was perfectly all right at home but would be a horrible embarrassment if seen by *yoso no hito*.

In the outside world — the *hakujin* world — there was a watchdog at work who rigorously edited out Japanese words and mannerisms when she spoke. Her words became formal, carefully chosen and somewhat artificial. She never thought they conveyed what she really felt, what she really was, because what she really was was unacceptable. In the realm of behavior, the watchdog was a tyrant. Respectability, as defined by popular novels and Hollywood heroines, must be upheld at all costs. How could she explain about the young men lounging in the doorways of her home and drinking in the back room with her father? How could she admit to the stories of the immigrant women who came to her mother desperate for protection from the beatings by their frenzied husbands? It was all so far from the drawing rooms of Jane Austen and the virtue and gallantry of Hollywood. The Japanese who passed through her house could drink, gamble, and philander, but she would never acknowledge it. She could admit to no weakness, no peculiarity. She would be irreproachable. She would be American.

Poverty was irreproachably American in the Depression years. Her father's oriental art goods business on Union Square had survived the 1906 earthquake only to be done in by the dishonesty of a *hakujin* partner who absconded with the gross receipts and the company car. The family survived on piecework and potatoes. Her mother organized a group of immigrant ladies to crochet window-shade rings. They got a penny apiece from the stores on Grant Avenue. Her father strung plastic birds onto multi-colored rings. As they sat working in the back room day after day, they must have dreamed of better times. They had all gambled the known for the unknown when they left Japan to come to America. Apparently it took more than hard work. They could work themselves to death for pennies. Entrepreneurial ventures were risky. They wanted to spare their sons and daughters this insecurity and hardship. Education was the key that would open the magical doors to a better future. Not that they hadn't been educated in Japan, indeed some of them were better educated than the people whose houses they cleaned on California Street. But they felt the key was an American education, a college education. Immigrant sons and immigrant daughters would fulfill their dreams.

She and her peers acquiesced in this dream. After all, wasn't it the same as their own? To succeed, to be irreproachable, to be American? She would be a smart career girl in a tailored suit, beautiful and bold — an American girl.

After the Depression her father opened a novelty store on Grant Avenue, and she was able to go to college. She set forth into the unknown with a generation of immigrant sons and daughters, all fortified by their mutual vision of the American dream.

They did everything right. They lived at home to save expenses. Each morning they woke up at dawn to catch the bus to the ferry building. They studied on the ferry as it made the bay crossing, and studied on the train from the Berkeley marina to Shattuck Avenue, a few blocks from the majestic buildings of the University of California. They studied for hours in the isolation of the library on campus. They brought bag lunches from the dark kitchens of old Japantown flats and ate on the manicured grass or at the Japanese Students' Club off campus. They went to football games and rooted for the home team. They wore bobby socks and Cal sweaters. The women had pompadours and the men parted their hair in the middle. They did everything correctly. But there was one thing they did not do: they did not break out of the solace of their own society to establish contact with the outside world.

In a picture dated 1939 of the graduating members of the Nisei Students' Club, there are about sixty of them in caps and gowns standing before California Hall. She is there, among the others, glowing triumphantly. No whisper of Pearl Harbor to cast a shadow on those bright faces. Yet all these young graduates would soon be clerking in Chinatown shops or pruning American gardens. Their degrees would get them nowhere, not because they hadn't done right, but because it was 1939 and they had Japanese faces. There was nowhere for them to go.

When the war came, her application for a teaching job had already been on file for two years. Since graduation she had been helping at her father's Grant Avenue store. Now she had to hand-letter signs for the store saying "Bargain Sale: Everything Must Go." Her father's back slumped in defeat as he watched the business he had struggled to build melt away overnight. America was creating a masterpiece and did not want their color.

They packed away everything they could not carry. Tom the Greek, from whom they rented Pine, promised to keep their possessions in the basement, just in case they would be able to come back someday. The quilts of bright

Japanese cloth, Imari dishes hand-carried by her mother from Japan, letters, photos, window-shade rings made in hard times, a copy of her junior college newspaper in which she had written a column, her Cal yearbook, faded pictures of bright Hollywood starlets — she put all her dreams in boxes for indefinite keeping. As they were told, they took along only what was practical, only what would serve in the uncertain times to come — blankets, sweaters, pots, and pans. Then, tagged like baggage, they were escorted by the U.S. Army to their various pick-up points in the city. And when the buses took them away, it was as though they had never been.

They were taken to Tanforan Racetrack, south of the city, which was to be their new home. The stables were used as barracks, and horse stalls became "apartments" for families. As she viewed the dirt and manure left by the former occupants, she realized, "So this is what they think of me." Realization was followed by shame. She recalled how truly she had believed she was accepted, her foolish confidence, and her unfounded dreams. She and her *nisei* friends had been spinning a fantasy world that was unacknowledged by the larger fabric of society. She had been so carried away by the aura of Berkeley that she had forgotten the legacy left her by Eleanor Leland. Now, the damp, dusty floor and stark cots reminded her sharply of her place. She was twenty-four. They lived in Tanforan for one year.

After a year they were moved to the Topaz Relocation Center in the wastelands of Utah. Topaz, Jewel of the Desert, they called it sardonically. Outside the barbed wire fence, the sagebrush traced aimless patterns on the shifting gray sands. Her sister Keiko could not endure it; she applied for an office job in Chicago and left the camp. Her brother enrolled at a midwestern university. She stayed and looked after her parents.

After a time she began to have trouble with her hearing. At first, it was only certain frequencies she could not hear, like some desert insects. Then it was even human voices, particularly when there was background noise. She couldn't be sure, but sometimes she wondered if it was a matter of choice, that if she only concentrated, she would be able to hear what someone was saying. But the blowing dust seemed to muffle everything anyway.

She left camp only once, and briefly, to marry the young man who had courted her wordlessly in the prewar days. He was a *kibei*, born in America and taken back to Japan at the age of eight. He had then returned to San Francisco to seek his fortune at the age of eighteen. He got off the boat with seven dollars in his pocket. He was one of those restless, lonely young men who would hang out at the Japantown pool hall, work at odd jobs by day, and go to school at night. He lived with a single-minded simplicity that seemed almost brash to someone like her who had grown up with so many unspoken rules. He wanted this sophisticated, college-educated American girl to be his wife, and she was completely won over. So she got leave from camp, and he from his unit, which was stationed at Fort Bragg, and they met in Chicago to cast a humble line into the uncertain future, a line they hoped would pull them out of this war into another, better life. Then they each returned to their respective barracks.

As defeat loomed inevitable for Japan, more and more people were allowed to leave the camps. Some of them made straight for the Midwest or East Coast, where feelings did not run so high against their presence, but her family could think only of going back home. The longing for San Francisco had become so strong that there was no question as to where they would go when they were released. They went straight back to Pine, and their hearts fell when they saw the filth and damage caused by three years of shifting tenancy. But they set about restoring it nevertheless because it was the only thing left of their lives.

The three years that had passed seemed like wasted years. The experience had no connection to the rest of her life; it was like a pocket in time, or a loose string. It was as though she had fallen asleep and dreamed the experience. But there was certainly no time to think about that now; they were busy rebuilding their lives.

She was pregnant with her first child. Her husband pleated skirts at a factory that hired Japanese. Later he ventured into the wholesale flower business where the future might be brighter. His hours were irregular; he rose in the middle of the night to deliver fresh flowers to market. Her sister, who had come back from Chicago to rejoin the family, took an office job with the government. Her parents were too old to start over. Her father hired out to do day work, but it shamed him so much that he did not want anyone else to know.

Then she was busy with the babies, who came quickly, one after another, all girls. She was absorbed in their nursing and bodily functions, in the sucking, smacking world of babies. How could she take time to pick up the pieces of her past selves, weave them together into a pattern, when there were diapers to be changed and washed, bowel movements to be recorded, and bottles sterilized? Her world was made up of Linda's solicitude for her younger sister Cathy, Cathy's curiosity, and the placidity of the third baby Sharon. Then there was Jo, who demanded so much attention because of her frail health. The house was filled with babies. Her husband was restless, fiercely independent — he wanted to raise his family in a place of his own.

So they moved out to the Avenues, leaving the dark corridors and background music of mixed tongues for a sturdy little house in a predominantly *hakujin* neighborhood, where everyone had a yard enclosed by a fence.

When first their father, then their mother, died, Keiko also moved out of Pine and closed it up for good. The old Victorian was too big for one person to live in alone. But before all the old things stored away and forgotten in the basement were thrown out or given away, was there anything she wanted to keep? Just her college yearbook from Cal. That was all she could think of. She couldn't even remember what had been so important, to have been packed away in those boxes so carefully when the war had disrupted their lives. She couldn't take the time with four babies to sift through it all now. It would take days. No, just her yearbook. That was all.

Sealed off in her little house in the fog-shrouded Avenues, the past seemed like a dream. Her parents, the old Victorian, the shuffling of slippered guests, and the low mumble of Japanese, all gone from her life. Her college friends were scattered all over the country, or married and sealed off in their own private worlds. But she felt no sense of loss. Their lives, after all, were getting better. There was no time to look back on those days before the war. The girls were growing. They needed new clothes for school. She must learn to sew. Somer & Kaufman was having a sale on school shoes. Could she make this hamburger stretch for two nights?

Linda was a bright and obedient child. She was very much the big sister. Jo, the youngest, was volatile, alternating between loving and affectionate, and strong and stubborn. Sharon was a quiet child, buffered from the world on both sides by sisters. She followed her sister, Cathy, demanding no special attention. Cathy was friendly and fearless, an unredeemable tomboy. When she slid down banisters and bicycled down the big hill next to their house in the Avenues, her mother's eyes would narrow as if in recognition, watching her.

As a mother, she was without fault. Her girls were always neatly dressed and on time. They had decent table manners, remembered to excuse themselves and say thank you. They learned to read quickly and loved books because she always read to them. She chose the books carefully and refused to read them any slang or bad grammar. Her children would be irreproachable.

She conscientiously attended PTA meetings, although this was a trial for her. She wasn't able to tell people about her hearing problem; somehow she was unable to admit to such a deficiency. So she did her best, sometimes pretending to hear when she didn't, nodding her head and smiling. She wanted things to go smoothly; she wanted to appear normal.

Linda, Cathy, and Jo excelled in school and were very popular. Linda held class offices and was invariably the teacher's pet. "A nice girl," her teachers said. Cathy was outgoing and athletic, and showed great talent in art and design — "a beautiful girl," in her teachers' estimation. Jo was rebellious, read voraciously, and wrote caustic essays and satires. Teachers sometimes disliked her, but they all thought she was "intelligent." Sharon was termed "shy." Although she liked the arts, Cathy was the artist of the family. And though Sharon read quite a bit, Jo was thought of as the reader. Sharon was not popular like Linda, and of all the Terasaki girls, she had to struggle the hardest, often unsuccessfully, to make the honor roll. But all in all, the girls vindicated their mother, and it was a happy time, the happiest time of her life.

Then they were grown up and gone. They left one by one. The house emptied room by room until it seemed there was nothing but silence. She had to answer the phone herself now, if she heard it ring. She dreaded doing so because she could never be sure if she was hearing correctly. Sometimes she let the telephone ring, pretending not to be home. The one exception was when her sister called every night. Then she would exchange news on the phone for an hour.

When her daughters came home to visit she came alive. Linda was doing the right things. She had a nice Japanese-American boyfriend; she was graduating from college; and she was going to get married.

Cathy was a bit of a free spirit, and harder to understand. She wore her hair long and straight, and seldom came home from Berkeley. When she did she seemed to find fault. Why didn't her mother get a hearing aid? Did she enjoy being left out of the hearing world? But Cathy had friends, interesting friends, *hakujin* friends, whom she sometimes brought home with her. She moved easily in all worlds, and her mother's heart swelled with pride to see it.

Sharon sometimes came home, sometimes stayed away.

When she did come home she did not have much to say. She was not happy in school. She liked throwing pots and weaving.

Then there was Jo, who would always bring a book or notebook home, and whose "evil pen" would pause absently in midstroke when her mother hovered near, telling her little bits of information that were new since the last visit. Jo, whose thoughts roamed far away, would gradually focus on the little figure of her mother. She had led such a sheltered life.

And then Cathy had died, and her mother didn't even cry.

Linda sent pictures from Germany of their mother in front of Heidelberg Castle, cruising down the Rhine. "She's just like a young girl," her letters proclaimed triumphantly. "She's excited about everything." But when their mother came home she talked about her trip for about a week. Then the old patterns prevailed, as if the house were a mold. In a month, Germany seemed like another loose thread in the fabric of her life. When Jo visited two months later, her mother was once again effaced, a part of the house almost, in her faded blouse and shapeless skirt, joylessly adding too much seasoned salt to the dinner salad.

"If only," Jo wrote Linda facetiously, "we could ship her out to some exotic place every other month."

In the fall Jo went to New York to study. "I have to get away," she wrote Linda. "The last time I went home I found myself discussing the machine washability of acrylics with Mom. There has got to be more to life than that." In the spring she had her mother come for a visit. No trip to the top of the Empire State Building, no Staten Island ferry,

with Jo. She whisked her mother straight from Kennedy
Airport to her cramped flat in the Village, and no sooner
had they finished dinner than Jo's boyfriend, Michael, ar-
rived.

Her mother was gracious. "Where do you live, Michael?" she asked politely.

He and Jo exchanged looks. "Here," he said.

Despite her mother's anxiety about the safety of New
York streets, the two of them walked furiously in the dusk
and circled Washington Square several times, mother
shocked and disappointed, daughter reassuring. At the end
of an hour they returned to the flat for tea, and by the end of
the evening the three of them had achieved an uneasy
truce.

"I knew you wouldn't be happy about it," Jo said to her,
"but I wanted you to know the truth. I hate pretending."

"Things were different when we were your age," her
mother said. "What's Daddy going to say?"

She stayed for two weeks. Every morning Michael
cooked breakfast, and the three of them ate together. Her
attitude toward the situation softened from one of guarded
assessment to tentative acceptance. Michael was very ar-
ticulate, Jo as level-headed as ever. Their apartment was
clean and homey. She began to relax over morning coffee at
the little round table by the window.

She remembered the trip she made to Chicago during
the war to get married. She had traveled from Topaz to
Chicago by train. It was her first trip alone. Her parents and
camp friends had seen her off at Topaz, and her sister and
future husband had met her at the station in Chicago. But
as the train followed its track northeastward across the
country, she had been alone in the world. She remembered

vividly the quality of light coming through the train window, and how it had bathed the passing countryside in a golden wash. Other passengers had slept, but she sat riveted at the window. Perhaps the scenery seemed so beautiful because of the bleakness and sensory deprivation of Topaz. She didn't know why she remembered it now.

Jo took her to the Metropolitan and to the Statue of Liberty. In a theater on Broadway they sat in the front row to see Deborah Kerr, her all-time favorite, and afterwards she declared she had heard every word.

When she left she shook Michael's hand and hugged Jo, saying, "I'll talk to Daddy."

But by the time Jo came home to visit a year later, the house, or whatever it was, had done its work. Her mother was again lost to her, a sweet little creature unable to hear very well, relaying little bits of information.

"I give up," said Jo. "We seem to lose ground every time. We dig her out, then she crawls back in, only deeper."

Linda loyally and staunchly defended the fortress in which her mother seemed to have taken refuge.

Jo wanted to break through. "Like shock treatment," she said. "It's the only way to bring her out."

Sharon, the middle daughter, gave her mother a loom.

And so, late in life, she took up weaving. She attended a class and took detailed notes, then followed them step by step, bending to the loom with painstaking attention, threading the warp tirelessly, endlessly winding, threading, tying. She made sampler after sampler, using the subdued, muted colors she liked: five inches of one weave, two inches of another, just as the teacher instructed.

For a year she wove samplers, geometric and repetitious, all in browns and neutral shades, the colors she preferred. She was fascinated by some of the more advanced techniques she began to learn. One could pick up threads from the warp selectively, so there could be a color on the warp that never appeared in the fabric if it were not picked up and woven into the fabric. With this technique she could show a flash of color, repeat flashes of the color, or never show it at all. The color would still be there, startling the eye when the piece was turned over. The back side would reveal long lengths of a color that simply hadn't been picked up from the warp and didn't appear at all in the right side of the fabric.

She took to her loom with new excitement, threading the warp with all the shades of her life: gray, for the cold, foggy mornings when she had warmed Jo's clothes by the heater vent as Jo, four, stood shivering in her pajamas; brown, the color of the five lunch bags she had packed each morning with a sandwich, cut in half and wrapped in waxed paper, napkin, fruit, and potato chips; dark brown, like the brownies they had baked "to make Daddy come home" from business trips. Sharon and Jo had believed he really could smell them, because he always came home.

Now when the daughters came home they always found something new she had woven. Linda, back from Germany, dropped by often to leave her daughter, Terry, at "*Bachan*'s house" before dashing off to work. When Linda's husband picked her up, Terry never wanted to leave "Bachi" and would cling to her, crying at the door.

She continued to weave: white, the color of five sets of sheets, which she had washed, hung out, and ironed each week — also the color of the bathroom sink and the lather of shampoo against four small black heads; blue, Cathy's favorite color.

Sharon came by from time to time, usually to do a favor or bring a treat. She would cook Mexican food or borrow a tool or help trim trees in the garden. She was frustrated with the public school system where she had been substitute teaching and was now working part time in a gallery.

Sometimes Sharon brought yarn for her mother to weave: golden brown, the color of the Central Valley in summer. The family had driven through the valley on their way to the mountains almost every summer. They would arrive hot and sweating and hurry into the cool, emerald green waters of the Merced River. The children's floats flashed yellow on the dark green water. Yellow, too, were the beaten eggs fried flat, rolled, and eaten cold, with dark brown pickled vegetables and white rice balls. She always sat in the shade.

Jo was working abroad and usually came home to visit once a year. She and Michael had broken up. During the visits the house would fill with Jo and her friends. They would sit in the back room to talk. Jo visited her mother's weaving class and met her weaving friends.

"So this is the daughter," one of them said. "Your mother's been looking forward to your visit. The only time she misses class is when her daughters are home."

Soon it was time for Jo to leave again. "Mom's colors," she remarked to Sharon as she fingered the brown muffler her mother had woven for her.

"Put it on," said Sharon.

Jo did, and as she moved toward the light, hidden colors leaped from the brown fabric. It came alive in the sunlight.

"You know, there's actually red in here," she marveled,

"and even bits of green. You'd never know it unless you looked real close."

"Most people don't," Sharon said.

The two sisters fell silent, sharing a rare moment together before their lives diverged again. Their mother's muffler was warm about Jo's neck.

At the airport, Jo's mother stood next to Jo's father, leaning slightly toward him as an object of lighter mass naturally tends toward a more substantial one. She was crying.

When Jo was gone she returned to the house, and her loom. And amidst the comings and goings of the lives around her, she sat, a woman bent over a loom, weaving the diverse threads of life into one miraculous, mystical fabric with timeless care.

INDEPENDENCE

I n the summer of '64 I was eleven.
I had just finished my first semester of junior high. My eldest sister, Linda, was spending her last summer at home before going away to college, to the big wide world of Berkeley that lay just across the bay. She was working at the Franchise Tax Board, and saving money. My other two sisters, Cathy and Sharon, were in the tenth and ninth grades, and yearned for adventure and romance, preferably on the beach.

I was a lowly preteen, and was perfectly content to loaf the summer away reading, hanging out with friends, and swimming at the Y. Cathy and Sharon, in their advanced years, wanted to go away.

Of course there were certain obstacles. The most apparent of these to my sisters was that Mom and Daddy would never let them just take off. Then there was the question of money. My sisters had none to speak of.

"Besides," Cathy complained, "how would we get there?"

"Get where?" I asked.

"Wherever," she said. "I'll go absolutely anywhere. But we don't have any wheels."

The obstacles were so numerous that it looked as though their adventure would have to be postponed a few more years, at least until one of them was old enough to get her driver's license. But the more impossible the situation seemed, the more obsessed my sisters became, until they felt they would die if they didn't get away that summer.

One Saturday in early June, Cathy came triumphantly into the sun room where Sharon and I were sprawled reading Nancy Drew mysteries.

"This is it," she announced dramatically, waving a copy of the *Nichibei Times*.

"This is what?" I asked.

"This is our summer vacation. Listen to this: 'Young man, for housework at Lake Tahoe cabin. July-August.'" She was ecstatic.

"I don't get it," I said. "What does that have to do with you?"

"It's perfect," she said. "Sharon and I can do housework. And a cabin! At Lake Tahoe! I mean, how much housework can there be? We can go to the beach every day!"

I hated to spoil her fun, but I was immediately struck by several glaring inconsistencies. First of all, I had serious reservations about my sisters' qualifications to do housework, but I thought I would pass over that as Cathy was sometimes prone to fits of violent temper. I proceeded to the next objection on my list.

"It says 'young man.' Did you notice that?"

"Man, woman, what's the difference? We're young, all right." Cathy was an optimist.

"Yeah, but there's two of you. It says 'man.' Singular."

"You take things too literally, Jo. Just think, they can get two of us for the price of one. They'll jump at the chance."

They began by approaching my mother, who could usually be won over, and whose aid could then be enlisted in approaching my father. Looking back on it, I'm amazed my father even listened to the proposition. It must have been my sisters' determination. Never once did they consider that the job might fall into other hands; if my dad said yes, it was theirs. He could not disappoint them, but neither would he allow them to go off into the unknown. He would find out the details first.

The details served to fire my sisters to greater heights of anticipation. The cabin was the property of Dr. Cluett, of San Francisco, but only his wife would be occupying it during the summer. The cabin was on the North Shore of Lake Tahoe, about two miles from the town of Homewood. The two girls would do light housekeeping chores and cooking (I was aghast) in return for their own room, board, and afternoons free. Cathy would receive sixty dollars for the six-week period; Sharon, as the younger, would receive fifty. My dad arranged for an interview. He wanted to check the lady out.

The Cluetts lived in Pacific Heights, and we drove by their house, days before the interview, to check it out. It was a very respectable-looking mansion.

When my sisters came home with my dad after the interview, they were ecstatic. Daddy had felt Mrs. Cluett to be trustworthy. Cathy and Sharon were to appear at the Cluett cabin on the first Saturday in July, in the early afternoon.

I felt betrayed, now that my sisters' departure was a reality. Here I had looked forward to a long summer of their companionship while engaging in traditional summer rituals: sprawling on the stairway with a stack of mysteries, snacking on Cap'n Crunch cereal (we had just discovered it and were addicted), listening to Giants games in the sun room, and knitting. And now my sisters were going off to have a great adventure. It was no fun listening to Giants games by yourself.

My parents made Linda promise to move into the bedroom that I usually shared with Sharon so that I would not feel too deserted; and so I cheered up somewhat at the prospect of a summer-long slumber party.

The night before the great adventure was to begin, my mother stayed up preparing our traditional family vacation picnic lunch of teriyaki Spam, rice balls, and potato salad. Early the next morning, we got up and left for Lake Tahoe. Cathy and Sharon had spent the week packing. After all the fuss and bother, I was amazed by how small their suitcases looked in the trunk of my dad's car. My dad also loaded the ice chest, the lunch, and the folding picnic table, which we were convinced was jinxed because every time we took it out, it would rain. And we were off.

We had our lunch by the lake, and sure enough, as soon as we had unpacked the picnic table, large raindrops began to fall. We finished eating in the car, and set out for the north shore.

We went several miles past Homewood before we decided we must have missed the turnoff. We turned around. Cathy and Sharon were silent.

It took several passes, back and forth, before my sharp-eyed mother spotted the Cluetts' name on a large tree, in an area that was so dense with trees that we had not thought people would live there. My dad turned in, and several trees deep we found ourselves in front of the Cluett cabin.

A young Japanese man came out to greet us.

"Terasaki-san?" he inquired. He introduced himself as Noguchi, Mrs. Cluett's houseboy.

I had never seen a real houseboy before — only on TV, so I studied him carefully. He was a lot younger than the ones on TV — probably in his early twenties. He didn't look like the houseboys on television. He wasn't subservient, sinister, or stupid. In short, I was rather disappointed. He just looked like a regular Japanese person. In fact, I thought he was rather cute. I looked at Linda, to see if she thought so, too. I could usually tell when she thought a guy was cute. She would start to act weird. But Linda didn't even seem to notice Noguchi.

Then Mrs. Cluett came out. She was a large, middle-aged woman. She did not smile. "Would you like to see your room?" she said.

I noticed Cathy craning her neck around as we entered the cabin. I thought she must be looking for the lake, which was nowhere in sight.

The trees were particularly dense around the cabin, and that, on top of the rainy weather, gave the cabin a dark, gloomy atmosphere. There was a cold, damp smell when we entered.

I watched Cathy and Sharon carefully. They were ominously silent.

One by one, we followed Mrs. Cluett up the stairs.

"Nice wood," I said.

"This will be your room," Mrs. Cluett said, opening a door onto a narrow chamber with bunk beds against one wall.

"Bunk beds! How neat!" I cried. We had always wanted bunk beds. "Look, Cathy — bunk beds!"

"Oh boy," she said, but she didn't sound too enthusiastic.

In fact, Cathy and Sharon didn't say anything until we were leaving. Mrs. Cluett asked us to give Noguchi a ride back to the city. He was leaving her employment, and had some friends in San Francisco. Noguchi got into the front seat with my dad. My mother got into the back with Linda and me.

Linda and I were dismayed. There was nothing like the presence of a total stranger to ruin the fun of a family car trip, especially this stranger, who seemed straight from Japan, very stiff and formal. He didn't even speak much English.

As my dad started the engine, Cathy and Sharon managed to say good-bye.

"See you in six weeks," Cathy said, as if she were already counting them.

It must have been hard for my dad to drive away and leave them there, but he did.

Noguchi and my dad conversed for a while in Japanese, but even that was hard going, and after a few of his pleasant inquiries were met with monosyllabic replies, my dad lapsed into silence. Linda and I were glad Noguchi was sitting in the front seat; we could make faces at each other behind his back. It was going to be a long trip.

We stopped halfway for A&W root beers. Noguchi loosened up some, and my dad explained to us that he was from Yokohama, and had been in the States for three months. He wanted to improve his English and go into business here, but he missed Japan. He had heard that being a houseboy was a good way to learn English, but he just couldn't get used to taking orders from a woman. He would have to find another job. I felt more kindly toward him when I heard he was homesick, and vowed to stop making faces whenever he did something weird. Linda looked as if she felt badly about it, too, but when he took one sip of his root beer and said it tasted more like medicine than beer, we forgot about kindness and exchanged looks of utter disgust.

When we got to the city, we dropped Noguchi off in front of a house on Sacramento Street. A friend lived there, he said.

My dad told him we would wait to make sure his friend was home, but Noguchi insisted that it wasn't necessary. He thanked us for the ride. My dad gave him our telephone number, and told him to come over on Thanksgiving.

"*Gambatte, ne*," my dad said. "Don't give up."

Noguchi stood on the sidewalk, bowing after us as we drove away.

"His friend must be rich," I said, looking back at the large Victorian in front of which Noguchi, growing smaller, remained standing.

"I wonder if he really has a friend living there," my dad said.

"What do you mean?" Linda asked.

My dad didn't answer.

"Why did you invite him to Thanksgiving?" I asked. "We don't even know him."

My dad seemed surprised by the question, and searched for an answer.

"It's hard to be away from home," he said finally.

"Do you think he'll really come?" I asked. I didn't think I would go to a strange family's house for Thanksgiving.

"He might," my dad said, "if he's doing well. Otherwise, he'll probably *enryo*. That's the way Japanese people are."

The summer resumed for me with swimming, reading, and writing an occasional letter to Cathy and Sharon. We got letters from them, telling of afternoons on the beach, which wasn't far from the cabin, and of walks into Homewood to pick up their mail. They would stop at the general store for a milkshake. They spent most nights in their room, talking and reading movie magazines. That sounded wonderful. Our mother had a low opinion of movie magazines, and to be able to read all the movie magazines you wanted to sounded like paradise.

Cathy's letters became humorous. They had begun calling Mrs. Cluett "Plicket," an abbreviation for "picky Cluett." She wanted everything done just so. Her patio furniture had to be moved every time it looked like rain, and moved back again when the sky cleared. Her rugs had to be continually beaten out. She went after bluejays with a BB gun, much to my sisters' amusement at first, then disgust, as the novelty wore off.

The letters became increasingly contemptuous, dark. Plicket washed her hair every day and pin-curled it, and it was like steel wool. Their "beach" was rocky, and frequented by packs of slobbering dogs.

At the end of three weeks, there was a phone call. I answered it, and was surprised to hear Sharon's voice.

"Hey, what's happening?" I said.

Her voice broke and I realized that she was crying. I listened, shocked, as there were scuffling noises and Cathy came on the line.

"Hey, Jo — how's it going? Listen — let me talk to Daddy."

I knew it was serious. I got my dad. My mom and Linda

gathered around the phone. My dad made several one-word replies, then concluded, "All right. We'll come get you this Saturday. You wanna talk to Mommy?"

I was incredulous. There must be forces at work in the world that I could not imagine, much less comprehend, forces that could overcome even big sisters. It was an occasion for solemnity.

The following Saturday we packed our picnic table and my mom's lunch, and set out again for the Cluett cabin. When we got there, Cathy and Sharon came out immediately with their suitcases. Mrs. Cluett came out to see them off.

"Thank you, Mrs. Cluett," Cathy said politely. She got into the car after Sharon. "Let's get out of here."

We drove into Homewood so that Cathy and Sharon could stop to check their mail one last time.

"There's the post office," Sharon said.

"And that's the general store where we used to get milkshakes," Cathy added. Though anxious to leave, they also wanted us to know the town as they did.

I looked around at the post office and the general store, the sidewalks of raised wooden slats like in an old cowboy movie. So this had been the scene of their independence.

They went into the general store for the last time. When they came out, Sharon handed me a brown paper bag.

"Look what we found," she said.

There was a box of Cap'n Crunch cookies inside.

"Try 'em," she said. "They're real good."

"Later," Cathy said. "Let's get out of here."

We stopped to have lunch along the Truckee River. My dad got out his fishing pole as Cathy got the old picnic table out of the trunk and set it up under a tree. When the rain started coming down, we just kept right on eating and fishing. When you're eating and fishing, what's a little rain?

Cathy and Sharon never did talk much about their summer at Lake Tahoe. I never found out what it was that had made their summer with Plicket so unbearable. They both knew, or perhaps they didn't know either, at least in so many words; so the experience remained locked within the silence of their deepest understanding. All they had chosen to share with me were the good things: the Cap'n Crunch cookies, the movie magazines, and memories of chocolate milkshakes. And my dad was right about Noguchi — when Thanksgiving came around that year, he didn't call. We wondered if he had stuck it out, and had his own business somewhere, or if he had gone back to Japan.

At the end of that summer Linda went away to Berkeley, and within the next six years, we all followed in her footsteps. In her junior year at Cal, Cathy, still pursuing a yen for adventure, fell to her death while rock-climbing. Years later, when I saw a vending machine selling Cap'n Crunch cookies in the empty corridor of an impersonal university building, I bought them immediately. And for a magical moment I was eleven years old again, feeling my sisters' love.

FIRST

LOVE

It was William Chin who started the rumor. He had been crossing California Street on a Saturday afternoon in December when he was almost struck down by two people on a Suzuki motorcycle. As if it weren't enough to feel the brush of death on the sleeve of his blue parka, a split second before the demon passed, he had looked up and caught sight of two faces he never would have expected to see on the same motorcycle — one of which he wouldn't have expected to see on a motorcycle at all. No one would have imagined these two faces exchanging words, or thought of them in the same thought even; yet there they were, together not only in physical space, but in their expressions of fiendish abandon as they whizzed by him. He was so shaken, first by his nearness to death, then by seeing an F.O.B. hood like Hideyuki "George" Sakamoto in the company of a nice girl like Joanne Terasaki, that it was a full five minutes before he realized, still standing in amazement on the corner of California and Fourth, that Joanne had been driving.

When William Chin's story got around, there was a general sense of outrage among the senior class of Andrew Jackson High — the boys, because an upstart newcomer like George Sakamoto had done what they were too shy to do (that is, he had gotten Joanne to like him), and the girls, because George Sakamoto was definitely cool and Joanne Terasaki, as Marsha Aquino objected with utter contempt, "doesn't even like to dance." Joanne's friends remained loyal and insisted that Jo would come to her senses by graduation. George's motorcycle cronies were less generous. "Dude's fuckin' crazy," was their cryptic consensus. Opinions differed as to which of the two lovers had completely lost their minds; however, it was unanimously held that the pairing was unsuitable.

And indeed, the two were from different worlds.

Hideyuki Sakamoto ("George" was his American name) was Japanese, a conviction that eight years, or half his life, in the States had failed to shake. He had transferred into Jackson High's senior class that year from wherever it was that F.O.B.s (immigrants fresh off the boat) transferred from; and though perhaps in his case the "fresh" no longer applied, the fact that he had come off the boat at one time or another was unmistakable. It lingered — rather, persisted — in his speech, which was ungrammatical and heavily accented, and punctuated by a mixture of exclamations commonly used on Kyushu Island and in the Fillmore District.

An F.O.B. at Jackson High could follow one of two routes: he could be quietly good at science or mathematics, or he could be a juvenile delinquent. Both options condemned him to invisibility. George hated math. His sympathies tended much more toward the latter option; however, he was not satisfied to be relegated to that category either. One thing was certain, and that was that George wanted no part of invisibility. As soon as his part-time job at Nakamura Hardware in Japantown afforded him the opportunity, he went out and acquired a second-hand Suzuki chopper (most hoods dreamed of owning a Harley, but George was Japanese and proud of it). He acquired threads which, when worn on his tall, wiry frame, had the effect — whether from admiration, derision, or sheer astonishment — of turning all heads, male and female alike. He had, in a short span of time, established a reputation as a "swinger."

So when William Chin's story got around about George Sakamoto letting Joanne Terasaki drive his bike, the unanimous reaction among the girls who thought of themselves as swingers was voiced by Marsha Aquino: "God dog, what a waste."

Joanne Terasaki, or "Jo," as she preferred to be called, was, in popular opinion, a "brain." Although her parents were living in Japantown when she was born, soon afterwards her grandparents had died and the family moved out to "the Avenues." Jo was a product of the middle-class, ethnically mixed Richmond District. She had an air of breeding that came from three generations of city living, one college-educated parent, and a simple belief in the illusion so carefully nurtured by her parents' generation, who had been through the war, that she was absolutely Mainstream. No one, however, would have thought of her in conjunction with the word "swing," unless it was the playground variety. Indeed, there was a childlike quality about her, a kind of functional stupidity that was surprising in a girl so intelligent in other respects. She moved slowly, as if her mind were always elsewhere, a habit that boys found mysterious and alluring at first, then exasperating. Teachers found it exasperating as well, even slightly insulting, as she earned As in their classes almost as an afterthought. Her attention was like a dim but powerful beacon, slowly sweeping out to sea for — what? Occasionally it would light briefly on the world at hand, and Jo would be quick, sharp, formidable. Then it would turn out to faraway places again. Perhaps she was unable to reconcile the world around her, the world of Jackson High, with the fictional worlds where her love of reading took her. In her mind, she was Scarlett O'Hara, Lizzy Bennet, Ari Ben Canaan. Who would not be disoriented to find oneself at one moment fleeing the Yankees through a burning Atlanta, and the next moment struggling across the finish line in girls' P.E.? Tart repartee with Mr. Darcy was far more satisfying than the tongue-tied and painful exchanges with boys that occurred in real life. Rebuffed boys thought Jo a snob, a heartless bitcn. The world of Andrew Jackson High was beneath her, that was it — a passing annoyance to be endured until she went out into the wider world and entered her true element. It must be on this wider world, this future glory, that her vision was so inexorably fixed.

Or perhaps it was fixed on a point just across San Francisco Bay, on the imposing campanile of the Berkeley campus of the University of California. She had always known she would go there, ever since, as a child, she had often gone to her mother's dresser and surreptitiously opened the top drawer to take out the fuzzy little golden bear bearing the inscription in blue letters, "CAL." It was one of the few "heirlooms" that her mother had salvaged from the wartime relocation. She had taken it with her to internment camp in the Utah desert, an ineffectual but treasured symbol of a shattered life. The government could take away her rights, her father's business, her home, but they could never take away the fact that she was U.C. Berkeley, Class of '39. Jo would have that, too. People often said of Jo that she was a girl who was going places; and they didn't mean on the back (or front) of George Sakamoto's bike.

Only love or drama could bring together two people cast in such disparate roles. When auditions began for the play that was traditionally put on by the senior class before

graduation, Jo, tired of being typecast as a brain, tried out
for the part most alien to her image — that of the brazen
hussy who flings herself at the hero in vain. For a brief moment she stood before her fellow classmates and sang her
way out of the cramped cage that their imaginations had
fashioned for her. The moment was indeed brief. Marsha
Aquino got the part.

"You have to admit, Jo," said William Chin apologeti-
cally, "Marsha's a natural." And Jo agreed, somewhat ma-
liciously, that Marsha was.

George, for his part, went for the lead. It was unheard of
for a hood (and an F.O.B., at that) to aspire to the stage,
much less the leading part. So thoroughly did George's as-
pect contradict conventional expectations of what a male
lead should be, that the effect was quite comic. His good-
natured lack of inhibition so charmed his audience that
they almost overlooked the fact that his lines had been un-
intelligible. At the last moment, a voice of reason prevailed,
and George was relegated to a nonspeaking part as one of
six princes in a dream ballet, choreographed by Jo's friend
Ava.

And so the two worlds converged.

"Grace," Ava was saying. "And — flair." She was putting the dream princes and princesses through their paces.
"This is a ballet."

The dancers shuffled about self-consciously. After
hours of work the princes and princesses, trained exclu-
sively in soul, were managing to approximate a cross between a square dance and a track-and-field event.

"You've got to put more energy into it, or something,"
Jo, who was a princess, observed critically as a sheepish

William Chin and Ed Bakowsky leaped halfheartedly across the floor.

"Like this, man!" George yelled suddenly, covering the stage in three athletic leaps. He landed crookedly on one knee, arms flung wide, whooping in exhilaration. There was an embarrassed silence.

"Yeah," Jo said. "Like that."

"Who is that?" she asked Ava after the rehearsal.

"I don't know," Ava said, "but what a body."

"That's George Sakamoto," said Marsha Aquino, who knew about everyone. "He's bad."

Jo, unfamiliar with the current slang, took her literally.

"Well, he seems all right to me. If it wasn't for him, our dream ballet would look more like 'The Funeral March.' Is he new?"

"He transferred from St. Francis," Marsha said. "That's where all the F.O.B.s go."

Jo had always had a vague awareness of Japanese people as being unattractively shy and rather hideously proper. Nothing could have been further from this image than George. Jo and her friends, most of whom were of Asian descent, were stunned by him, as a group of domesticated elephants born and bred in a zoo might have been upon meeting their wild African counterpart for the first time. George was a revelation to Jo, who, on the subject of ethnic identity, had always numbered among the ranks of the sublimely oblivious.

George, meanwhile, was already laying his strategy. He was not called "*Sukebe* Sakamoto" by his friends for nothing.

"This chick is the door-hanger type," he told his friend Doug. "You gotta move real slow."

"Yeah," Doug said. "Too slow for you."

"You watch, sucker."

He called her one weekend and invited her and Ava to go bowling with him and Doug. Jo was struck dumb on the telephone.

"Ha-ro, is Jo there?"

"This is Jo."

"Hey, man. This is George."

"Who?"

"George, man. Sakamoto."

"Oh." Then she added shyly, "Hi."

The idea of bowling was revolting, but Jo could bowl for love.

She told her mother that she had a date. Her mother mentally filed through her list of acquaintances for a Sakamoto.

"Is that the Sakamoto that owns the cleaner on Fillmore?"

"I don't think so," Jo said.

"Well, if Ava's going, I guess it's all right."

When George came to pick her up, Jo introduced him to her father, who was sitting in the living room watching television.

"Ha-ro," George said, cutting a neat bow to her startled father.

"Was that guy Japanese?" her father asked later when she returned.

"Yeah," Jo said, chuckling.

There was an unspoken law of evolution which dictated that in the gradual march toward Americanization, one did not deliberately regress by associating with F.O.B.s. Jo's mother, who was second generation, had endured much criticism from her peers for "throwing away a college education" and marrying Jo's father, who had graduated from high school in Japan. Even Jo's father, while certainly not an advocate of this law, assumed that most people felt this way. George, therefore, was a shock.

On their second date, Jo and George went to see Peter O'Toole in a musical. From then on, they decided to dispense with the formalities, a decision owing only in part to the fact that the musical had been wretched. The main reason was that they were in love.

They would drive out to the beach, or to the San Bruno hills, and sit for hours, talking. In the protective shell of George's mother's car they found a world where they were not limited by labels. They could be complex, vulnerable. He told her about his boyhood in Kyushu, about the sounds that a Japanese house makes in the night. He had been afraid of ghosts. His mother had always told him ghost stories. She would make her eyes go round and utter strange sounds: "*Ka-ra . . . ko-ro . . . ka-ra . . . ko-ro . . .* " —the sound made by the wooden sandals of an approaching ghost. Japanese ghosts were different from American ghosts, he said. They didn't have feet.

"If they don't have feet," Jo asked curiously, "how could they wear sandals?"

George was dumbfounded. The contradiction had never occurred to him.

They went for motorcycle rides along the roads that wound through the Presidio, at the edge of cliffs overlooking the Golden Gate. Then, chilled by the brisk winter fog, they would stop at his house in Japantown for a cup of green tea.

He lived in an old Victorian flat on the border between Japantown and the Fillmore, with his mother and grandmother and cat. His mother worked, so it was his grandmother who came from the kitchen to greet them. (But this was later. At first, George made sure that no one would be home when they went. He wanted to keep Jo a secret until he was sure of her.)

The Victorian kitchen, the green tea, all reminded Jo of her grandparents' place, which had stood just a few blocks away from George's house before it was torn down. Jo had a vague memory of her grandmother cooking fish in the kitchen. She couldn't remember her grandfather at all. The war had broken his spirit, taken his business, forced him to do day work in white people's homes, and he had died when Jo was two. After that, Jo's family moved out of Japantown, and she had not thought about the past until George's house reminded her. It was so unexpected, that the swinger, the hood, the F.O.B. George Sakamoto should awaken such memories.

But they eventually had to leave the protective spaces that sheltered their love. Then the still George of the parked car and Victorian kitchen, the "real" George, Jo wanted to believe, evolved, became the flamboyant George, in constant motion, driven to maintain an illusion that would elude the cages of other people's limited imaginations.

He took her to dances Jo had never known existed. Jo had been only to school dances, where everyone stood around too embarrassed to dance. The dances that George took her to were dark, crowded. Almost everyone was Asian. Jo knew no one. Where did all these people come from? They were the invisible ones at school, the F.O.B.s. They *dressed* (unlike Jo and her crowd, who tended toward corduroy jeans). And they danced.

George was in his element here. In his skintight striped slacks flared at the calf, black crepe shirt open to the navel, billowing sleeves and satiny white silk scarf, he shimmered like a mirage in the strobe lights that cut the darkness. Then, chameleonlike, he would appear in jeans and a white T-shirt, stocking the shelves of Nakamura Hardware. At school, George shunned the striped shirts and windbreaker jackets that his peers donned like a uniform. He wore turtleneck sweaters under corduroy blazers, starched shirts in deep colors with cuff links. When he rode his bike, he was again transformed, a wild knight in black leather.

"The dudes I ride with," George confided to Jo in the car, "see me working in the store, and they say, 'Hey, what is this, man? You square a-sup'm?' Then the guys in the store, they can't believe I hang out with those suckers on bikes. 'Hey George,' they say, 'you one crazy son-of-a-bitch.' In school, man, these straight suckers can't believe it when I do good on a test. I mean, I ain't no hot shit at English, but I ain't no dumb sucker neither. 'Hey George,' they say, 'you tryin' to get into college a-sup'm?' 'Hey, why not, man?' I say. They can't take it if you just a little bit different, you know? All them dudes is like that — 'cept you."

Jo was touched, and tried to be the woman of George's dreams. It was a formidable endeavor. Nancy Sinatra was the woman of George's dreams. For Christmas Jo got a pair of knee-high black boots. She wore her corduroy jeans tighter in the crotch.

"Hey, George," Doug said. "How's it goin' with Slow Jo?"

"None of your fuckin' business, man," George snapped.

"Oh-oh. Looks bad."

On New Year's Eve Jo discovered French kissing and thought it was "weird." She got used to it, though.

"You tell that guy," her father thundered, "that if he's gonna bring that motorcycle, he doesn't have to come around here anymore!"

"Jesus Christ!" Jo wailed, stomping out of the room. "I can't wait to get out of here!"

Then they graduated, and Jo moved to Berkeley in the spring.

The scene changed from the narrow corridors of Andrew Jackson High to the wide steps and manicured lawns of the university. George was attending a junior college in the city. He came over on weekends.

"Like good ice cream" he said. "I want to put you in the freezer so you don't melt."

"What are you talking about?"

They were sitting outside Jo's dormitory in George's car. Jo's roommate was a blonde from Colusa who had screamed the first time George walked into the room with Jo. ("Hey, what's with that chick?" George had later complained.)

"I want to save you," George said.

"From what?" Jo asked.

He tried another analogy. "It's like this guy got this fancy shirt, see? He wants to wear it when he goes out, man. He don't want to wear it every day, get it dirty. He wears an old T-shirt when he works under the car — get grease on it, no problem. It don't matter. You're like the good shirt, man."

"So who's the old T-shirt?" Jo asked, suddenly catching on.

"Hey, nobody, man. Nobody special. You're special. I want to save you."

"I don't see it that way," Jo said. "When you love someone, you want to be with them and you don't mind the grease."

"Hey, outasight, man."

So he brought her to his room.

George's room was next to the kitchen. It was actually the dining room converted into a young man's bedroom. It had the tall, narrow Victorian doors and windows, and a sliding door to the living room, which was blocked by bookshelves and a stereo. The glass-doored china cabinet, which should have housed Imari bowls, held tapes of soul music, motorcycle chains, Japanese comic books, and Brut. In Jo's grandparents' house there had been a black shrine honoring dead ancestors in the corner of the dining room. The same corner in George's room was decorated by a life-sized poster of a voluptuous young woman wearing skintight leather pants and an equally skintight (but bulging) leather jacket, unzipped to the waist.

George's mother and grandmother were delighted by Jo. In their eyes she was a "nice Japanese girl," something they never thought they would see, at least in conjunction with George. George had had a string of girlfriends before Jo, which had dashed their hopes. Jo was beyond their wildest expectations. It didn't seem to matter that this "nice Japanese girl" didn't understand any Japanese; George's grandmother spoke to her anyway, and gave her the benefit of the doubt when she smiled blankly and looked to George for a translation. They were so enthusiastic that George was embarrassed, and tried to sneak Jo in and out to spare her their effusions.

They would go to his room and turn up the stereo and make love to the lush, throbbing beat of soul. At first Jo was mortified, conscious of what her parents would say, knowing that "good girls" were supposed to "wait." But in the darkness of George's room, all of that seemed very far away.

So her first experiences of love were in a darkened room filled with the ghosts of missing Japanese heirlooms; in the spaces between the soul numbers with which they tried to dispel those ghostlike shadows, sounds filtered in from the neighboring kitchen: samurai music from the Japanese program on television, the ancient voice of his grandmother calling to the cat, the eternal shuffle of slippers across the kitchen floor. When his mother was home and began to worry about what they were doing in his room, he installed a lock, and when she began pounding on the door, insisting that it was getting late and that George really should take Jo home, George would call out gruffly, "Or-righ! Or-righ!"

But there was that other world, Jo's weekday world, a world of classical buildings, bookstores, coffee shops, and tear gas (for the United States had bombed Cambodia).

Jo flitted like a ghost between the two worlds so tenuously linked by a thin span of steel suspended over San Francisco Bay. She wanted to be still, and at home, but where? On quiet weekday mornings, reading in an empty courtyard with the stillness, the early morning sun, the language of Dickens, she felt her world full of promise and dreams. Then the sun rose high, people came out, and Jo and her world disappeared in a cloak of invisibility, like a ghost.

"Her English is so good," Ava's roommate remarked to Ava. "Where did she learn it?"

"From my parents," Jo said. "In school, from friends. Pretty much the same way most San Franciscans learn it, I guess."

Ava's roommate was from the East Coast, and had never had a conversation with an 'Oriental' before.

"She just doesn't know any better," Ava apologized later.

"Well where has that chick been all her life?" Jo fumed.

Then she would long for George, and he would come on the weekend to take her away. Locked together on George's bike, hurtling back and forth between two worlds, they found a place where they could be still and at peace.

George tried to be the man of her dreams. They went on hikes now instead of soul dances. He would appear in jeans and a work shirt, and he usually had an armload of books. He was learning to type, and took great pains over his essays for Remedial English.

But they began to feel the strain. It began to bother George that Jo made twenty-five cents an hour more at her part-time job in the student dining room than he did at the hardware store. He had been working longer. He needed the money. Jo, on the other hand, never seemed to buy anything. Just books. Although her parents could afford to send her to college, her high-school record had won her a scholarship for the first year. She lived in a dream world. She had it so easy.

He asked to borrow fifty dollars, he had to fix his car, and she lent it to him immediately. But he resented it, resented his need, resented her for having the money, for parting with it so easily. Everything, so easily. And he tortured her.

"Hey, is something wrong, man?" George asked suddenly, accusing, over the phone.

"Wrong?" Jo was surprised. "What do you mean?"

"You sound funny."

"What do you mean, funny?"

"You sound real cold, man," George said. His voice was flat, dull.

"There's nothing wrong!" Jo protested, putting extra emphasis in her voice to convince him, then hating herself for doing so. "I'm fine."

"You sound real far away," George went on, listlessly.

"Hey, is something bothering *you?*"

"No," George said. "You just sound funny to me. Real cold, like you don't care." He wanted her to be sympathetic, remorseful.

And at first she was — repentant, almost hysterical. Then she became impatient. Finally, she lapsed into indifference.

"I have the day off tomorrow," George said over the phone. "Can I come?"

Jo hesitated.

"I have to go to classes," she warned.

"That's okay," he said. "I'll come with you."

There was another long pause. "Well . . . we'll see," she said.

As soon as she saw him the next day, her fears were confirmed. He had gone all out. He wore a silky purple shirt open halfway to his navel, and skintight slacks that left nothing to the imagination. There was something pathetic and vulnerable about the line of his leg so thoroughly revealed by them. As they approached the campus, George pulled out a pair of dark shades and put them on.

He was like a character walking into the wrong play. He glowed defiantly among the faded jeans and work shirts of the Berkeley campus.

Jo's first class was Renaissance Literature.

"If you want to do something eise," she said, "I can meet you after class."

"That's okay, man," George said happily. "I want to see what they teaching you."

"It's gonna be real boring," she said.

"That's okay," he said. "I have my psych book."

"If you're going to study," Jo said carefully, "maybe you should go to the library."

"Hey," George said, "you tryin' to get rid of me?"

"No," Jo lied.

"Then let's go."

They entered the room. It was a seminar of about ten people, sitting in a circle. They joined the circle, but after a few minutes of discussion about *Lycidas,* George opened his psychology textbook and began to read.

Jo was mortified. The woman sitting on the other side of George was looking curiously, out of the corner of her eye, at the diagram of the human brain in George's book.

"Would you care to read the next stanza aloud?" the lecturer asked suddenly. "You — the gentleman with the dark glasses."

There was a horrible moment as all eyes turned to George, bent over his psychology textbook. He squirmed and sank down into his seat, as if trying to become invisible.

"I think he's just visiting," the woman next to George volunteered. "I'll read."

Afterwards, Jo was brutal. Why had he come to the class if he was going to be so rude? Why hadn't he sat off in the corner, if he was going to study? Or better yet, gone to the library as she had suggested? Didn't he know how inappropriate his behavior was? Didn't he care if they thought that Japanese people were boors? Didn't he know? Didn't he care?

No, he didn't know. He was oblivious. It was the source of his confidence, and that was what she had loved him for.

And so the curtain fell on their little drama, after a predictable denouement — agreeing that they would date others, then a tearful good-bye one dark night in his car, parked outside her apartment. Jo had always thought it somewhat disturbing when characters who had been left dead on the set in the last act, commanding considerable emotion by their demise, should suddenly spring to life not a minute later, smiling and bowing, and looking as unaffected by tragedy as it is possible to look. She therefore hoped she would not run into George, who would most certainly be smiling and bowing and oblivious to tragedy. She needn't have worried. Their paths had never been likely to cross.

Jo was making plans to study in New York when she heard through the grapevine that George was planning a trip to Europe. He went that summer, and when he returned, he brought her parents a gift. Jo's parents, who had had enough complaints about George when Jo was seeing him, were touched, and when Christmas came around Jo's mother, in true Japanese fashion, prepared a gift for George to return his kindness. Jo, of course, was expected to deliver it.

She had had no contact with him since they had broken up. His family was still living in Japantown, but the old Victorian was soon going to be torn down for urban renewal, and they were planning to move out to the Avenues, the Richmond District where Jo's parents lived.

As Jo's dad drove her to George's house, Jo hoped he wouldn't be home, hoped she could just leave the gift with his mother. She was thankful that she was with her father, who had a habit of gunning the engine as he sat waiting in the car for deliveries to be made, and was therefore the ideal person with whom to make a quick getaway.

George's grandmother opened the door. When she saw who it was, her face changed and she cried out with pleasure. Jo was completely unprepared for the look of happiness and hope on her face.

"Jo-chan!" George's grandmother cried; then, half-turning, she called out Jo's name twice more, as if summoning the household to her arrival.

Jo was stunned.

"This is for George," she said, thrusting the gift at George's grandmother, almost throwing it at her in her haste. "Merry Christmas."

She turned and fled down those stairs for the last time, away from the doomed Victorian and the old Japanese woman who stood in the doorway still, calling her name.

AMERICAN

FISH

Mrs. Hayashi was inspecting a daikon radish in the American Fish Market in Japantown when she recognized a woman who was heading toward the burdock roots.

I know her, she thought. What was her name? Suzuki? Kato? She decided to pretend not to see the woman, and see if the woman recognized her. She put down the radish and picked up another.

"Oh . . . hello," said the woman, who was now standing next to her.

Mrs. Hayashi looked up and smiled enthusiastically. "Oh, hi!" she said. "Long time no see." Immediately she regretted the remark. What if it was someone she had just seen yesterday?

"How've you been?" the woman asked.

"Fine, just fine," Mrs. Hayashi said. I should ask her about her husband, she thought. Did she have a husband?

"How's your husband?" the woman asked.

Mrs. Hayashi's husband had died ten years before. Obviously, the woman was someone she had not seen in quite some time. Thank goodness, she thought. Then it had been appropriate to say "long time no see."

"He passed away several years ago," Mrs. Hayashi said.

"Oh, so sorry to hear that," the woman said.

I should ask her about her children, Mrs. Hayashi thought. But since she still did not know if the woman had a husband or not, she couldn't very well assume that she had children. Wouldn't it be awful if I asked her about her children and it turned out she wasn't even married! And even if she was married, and did have children, what if they had died, or committed crimes? After all, everyone couldn't have a son in law school, and Mrs. Hayashi did not like to appear to be boasting. No, she'd better avoid the subject of children.

"How are your kids?" the woman asked.

"Oh, Bill is just fine," Mrs. Hayashi replied. She couldn't stand it. "He'll be graduating from law school next spring," she added, consoling herself with the thought that at least she had refrained from mentioning that her son was at the top of his class.

"That's nice," said the woman. "And what about your daughter?"

"I don't have a daughter," Mrs. Hayashi said stiffly. "Just a son." She was beginning to think that the woman wasn't anyone she knew very well.

"Stupid me," said the woman. "I was thinking of someone else."

"How are *your* children?" Mrs. Hayashi asked, throwing caution to the wind.

"Fine," the woman said. "Emily and her husband live in San Jose and have two little girls."

"How nice," Mrs. Hayashi said.

There was a pause. Mrs. Hayashi did not know anyone named Emily. Who was this woman?

It occurred to her that the woman might be someone she didn't like. How aggravating, she thought, not to be able to remember whether to be pleasant to someone or not.

"I'm so sorry," the woman said, "But I have a real bad memory for names. It was Suzuki-san, wasn't it?"

"Hayashi," Mrs. Hayashi said, peeved. "Grace Hayashi."

"Of course," said the woman, somewhat vaguely. "Hayashi . . ."

"And . . . forgive me," said Mrs. Hayashi, seizing the opportunity, "but you're . . . ?"

"Nakamura," the woman said. "Toshi Nakamura."

The name did not even ring a bell.

"Is that the family that runs the bakery on Fillmore?" Mrs. Hayashi asked.

"No," the woman said, "not that Nakamura."

"Then you must be related to Frank Nakamura."

"No."

"How odd," Mrs. Hayashi said without thinking, and was embarrassed when she realized she had spoken aloud.

"My maiden name was Fujii," Mrs. Nakamura said.

"Fujii . . ." Mrs. Hayashi said, thinking hard.

"Maybe you know my sister Eiko."

"Eiko Fujii . . ." Mrs. Hayashi said, frowning.

Then a horrible thought occurred to Mrs. Hayashi. Perhaps she did not know this woman at all; perhaps Mrs. Nakamura just looked like someone she knew, or someone she should know — a Japanese-American lady in her late fifties, the same age as Mrs. Hayashi, wearing a somewhat faded but sensible raincoat even though it was not raining outside. But then, Mrs. Nakamura had recognized her, too.

"Did I know you in Topaz?" Mrs. Hayashi asked.

"Oh, no," Mrs. Nakamura said. Mrs. Hayashi waited, but the other woman said nothing further.

"You weren't in Topaz?" Mrs. Hayashi continued.

"No."

"Where were you — Manzanar?" Mrs. Hayashi asked pleasantly.

"No."

"Oh, well," Mrs. Hayashi said, becoming flustered. "Perhaps you weren't in camp during the war. I don't mean to pry."

"I was in Tule Lake," Mrs. Nakamura said, turning to pick through the burdock roots. She rejected a shriveled bunch of roots and put a fresh bunch in her cart.

"Oh," Mrs. Hayashi said. She felt her face go hot. Tule Lake was where all those branded "disloyal" had been imprisoned during the war. "I see," Mrs. Hayashi said, searching for a way to change the topic.

"Do you?"

Mrs. Hayashi was startled. "I'm sorry," she said. "I don't know what you mean."

"And I don't know what you see," Mrs. Nakamura said.

"Nothing," Mrs. Hayashi said. "I just meant — oh."

"Oh," Mrs. Nakamura said.

Mrs. Hayashi by this time was extremely uncomfortable and groped for a way to redeem the situation.

"I knew some people who were in Tule Lake," she said. "The Satos. From Watsonville. Did you know them?"

"No," Mrs. Nakamura said.

"It was the silliest thing, really," Mrs. Hayashi went on. "Mr. Sato was a Buddhist priest, and after Pearl Harbor, his name got on some list, and the FBI picked him up. Imagine that."

Mrs. Nakamura was silent.

"As if being Buddhist was a crime," Mrs. Hayashi added, trying to make clear where her sympathies lay. She was not a Buddhist herself, but she thought Mrs. Nakamura might be one.

"My father said he wanted to go back to Japan," Mrs. Nakamura said suddenly. "That's why we were in Tule Lake."

"Oh," Mrs. Hayashi said.

"They took his boat away after Pearl Harbor," Mrs. Nakamura continued. "He was a fisherman down in Terminal Island. Without a boat, he couldn't make a living. He thought the only thing to do was to go back to Japan."

"I know," Mrs. Hayashi said. "My father was forced to sell his store to the first person who offered to buy. A lifetime of hard work, just thrown away!"

"It made my father mad," Mrs. Nakamura went on. "He said why stay in a country that doesn't want us?"

"That's perfectly logical," Mrs. Hayashi reassured. "Why indeed?"

"Why did *your* parents want to stay?" Mrs. Nakamura asked.

"Well," Mrs. Hayashi said, startled. "I don't know." She thought for a moment, then said, "I guess they knew that we, I mean my brothers and sisters and I, would never want to go to Japan. I mean, we were born here. We belonged here. And they wanted the family to stay together."

"That's how my mother and I felt," Mrs. Nakamura said. "That's why we said we wanted to go back to Japan, too — so we'd be all together. Except in those days, that made you disloyal."

"Well, it was ridiculous," Mrs. Hayashi said firmly. "And it caused so much grief."

There was a silence.

"Where did you go back to, in Japan?" Mrs. Hayashi asked gently.

"Oh, we didn't go back," Mrs. Nakamura replied cheerfully. "My father changed his mind when he remembered that they didn't have central heating in Japan."

Both women burst out laughing.

Mrs. Hayashi, still laughing, threw a bunch of burdock roots into her cart.

"Well, I should be getting along," Mrs. Nakamura said. "I'm so glad I bumped into you . . ." She stopped, embarrassed.

"Hayashi."

". . . Hayashi-san," she finished. "Now if I could just remember who you are."

They laughed again.

"I'm sure it'll come back to us," Mrs. Hayashi said. "Everything does."

"Do you go to the Buddhist church?" Mrs. Nakamura asked. "Maybe I've seen you there."

"I doubt it," Mrs. Hayashi replied. "I'm Methodist. But I've been to funerals at the Buddhist church, so maybe."

"That must be it — we must have met at someone's funeral," Mrs. Nakamura agreed. "I'm sure it'll come to me as soon as I walk out of here with my groceries. Isn't it always like that?"

"It can't be that mysterious," Mrs. Hayashi said. "I mean, our lives aren't so terribly complicated. If we didn't know each other in camp, then we knew each other before the war, or after the war. I'm sure I won't be able to sleep until I remember which it was," she added cheerfully. "I hate to forget things. That is, unless they're the sort of things you'd rather not remember."

Mrs. Nakamura looked at her watch.

"My goodness," she said. "I have to run. I have to be at work in an hour."

"Work?" Mrs. Hayashi said.

"Yes; I work at Macy's," Mrs. Nakamura said. "I'm in . . ."

"Gift wrap!" Mrs. Hayashi said, remembering.

The two women stared incredulously at each other for an instant, then broke into raucous laughter. Then they bowed slightly, and continued on their separate ways.

WILD

MUSHROOMS

When I was living in Japan, my father came to visit me. We went down to Hiroshima, looking for his old neighborhood.

It was February, but there was no snow on the ground. We took the Shinkansen that stopped in the city where I was living, which meant that it was a regular super express rather than a limited super express. It made all the super express stops. We didn't mind. We were taking a trip into the past; it was not necessary to hurry. We stopped in Atami, Mishima, Shizuoka, and I remembered the time before I had ever seen Japan when my father laid a map out on the diningroom table and put his finger on Odawara, my city.

"It's famous for *kamaboko*," he said.

Kamaboko, a kind of rubbery fish baloney, was not my favorite food, but I swore to try some when I got there.

His finger moved down the Tokaido Main Line.

"Atami . . . a famous resort," he said. "Lots of hot springs."

His finger next stopped on Hamamatsu.

"Their *unagi*," he said, "is the best."

He told me about the eel, commercially raised in Hamamatsu Bay and broiled in soy sauce, then served over rice in shaved wooden boxes at Hamamatsu Station.

When our train pulled into Hamamatsu Station, we were ready. A Japanese friend had told me that car number nine stopped directly in front of the eel box lunch stand. It was necessary to know this because the train stopped for exactly three minutes, and waited for no one. When the door opened, I dashed out to the stand, which was right where my friend had said it would be. There was something comforting about the predictability of life in

Japan. My father never dashed, but somehow he was right there with me, holding out three thousand-yen notes. We got our lunches and were back, settled comfortably in our seats, before the warning bell rang and the doors closed.

About Hiroshima, that time with the map in the dining room, all my father had said was, "It's famous for oysters." He never talked much about his past. He didn't talk much, period. And I didn't ask, because I always figured if people want to talk about something, they will. I couldn't see myself asking him, like an investigative reporter on television, "How did you feel when you heard that your mother had been killed in the atomic bombing?" She died in her home in the center of the city. At the time, my father was a private in the U.S. Army, stationed at Camp Shelby, Mississippi. How did he hear about the bombing of Hiroshima? From a newspaper? The radio?

After the war, my father's business trips took him to Japan about once a year, but to Yokohama or Osaka, never Hiroshima. Twice, he made special trips down to Hiroshima to see his sister, who had survived the atom bomb, but he went only to her shop in Hondori, the main shopping street, or to her home in the suburbs — never to the old neighborhood where he had lived for ten years after his family returned to Japan from America. This was his first visit since the death of his sister in 1970. She had died in a Tokyo hospital, twenty-five years after the end of the war, from disorders caused by radiation.

Like my grandmother's death in the atomic bombing or my mother's family's internment during the war, Japan seemed to have always been part of my consciousness. There was never a moment when I "found out" about it; it was no terrible secret, hidden, then discovered. It was always there, in the background, mysterious and compelling like a dark shape in a room at night which becomes clear only if the light is turned on it. Perhaps, in the beginning, it was just a smell — the smell of fresh straw mats or green tea emanating from my father's suitcase, which lay open in the entryway after his return from a business trip. It was a hot, damp smell, mildewy, which I found repulsive but fascinating. Or perhaps it was the gifts that filled his suitcases, wrapped in the white Takashimaya Department Store paper with pale red and gray roses: cans of tea, packages of dried squid, delicate writing paper with a faint imprint of cherry blossoms. Once there was a stuffed animal, a cat with the softest golden brown fur I had ever felt, and I thought Japan must be a terrific place. But the pictures my father brought back, of unsmiling men in dark suits, did not interest me. My father stood a head taller and looked as serious as they did — my father, who usually smiled or laughed in pictures unless he was mad. I thought at the time maybe Japan was not a place I wanted to go.

Yet here I was, throwing light on the dark shape that hovered over my sleep.

About five minutes before arriving at Hiroshima Station, our train flashed through a series of tunnels. I caught a glimpse of green wooded hills.

"We used to go hunting for *matsutake* in these hills," my father said. "Wild mushrooms."

Then we emerged from the last tunnel into the basin formed by hills that contained the city of Hiroshima. It was twilight. My attention was caught by a large building on a hillside. Its silver dome rose eerily above the city, reflecting the colors of the twilight.

"What is that?" I asked my father, pointing.

"I don't know," he said.

"It's beautiful."

In the morning we took a taxi from our hotel, the Hiroshima Grand, which of course had not been built in the days when my father lived there.

"Hakushima," my father instructed the driver.

We followed streetcar tracks away from the downtown area until we found ourselves in an undistinguished residential neighborhood.

"It was around here," my father said, instructing the driver to let us off at the corner. We got out, and I followed my father, who stopped at each corner, looked about uncertainly, and turned either right or left. One block from the main thoroughfare the streets narrowed. We meandered for several minutes. It was cold. The weather forecast had said maybe snow.

All I knew was that my grandparents had built a house in Hiroshima after returning from America. Their twenty-year sojourn in California was a prosperous one, and they were among the few Japanese in 1926 to have western-style beds in their house. My grandmother was certainly the only Japanese in town with a General Electric stove. But my grandfather died three years later, and one by one, my father's sisters married and moved out to the suburbs of Hiroshima. As soon as he turned eighteen, my father went back to America. When the bomb fell, my grandmother was alone in the house.

"I think there was a *sake* store around here," my father said. "A guy in my class, his parents ran it."

We turned another corner, and there was a small shop. We went in.

"*Irasshai-mase!*" called the shop owner, greeting us.

I browsed about the aisles, cataloguing the merchandise. Stacked boxes of tissue, tied together with plastic string. Laundry soap. Notebooks and envelopes. A kerosene heater glowed in one corner. My father was speaking to the owner. I understood a word here and there.

"Before..." my father was saying. "Here...liquor store?"

The owner sucked in deeply with a tilt of the head.

"*Saaahh*..." he sighed. "Around here...no liquor store."

"But," my father said, "...a long time ago...Before the war...?"

The shop owner smiled.

"I...after the war...came to Hiroshima," he said. He murmured more apologetic words I couldn't understand.

My father continued. "Family named Sakai...know them?" he asked.

"*Saaahh*..." the owner replied regretfully. "...don't know..."

There was a pause.

"Relatives?" the owner asked.

My father said something about school.

"*Dochira no kata desuka?*" the shop man asked.

"*A-me-ri-ka,*" my father answered. "*Ka-ri-hō-ru-ni-ya-shu.*"

"*Ah, sō desuka,*" the man said. Then, gently, "Completely...changed...isn't it?" He meant Hiroshima. He used the form that implied deduction rather than observation, since he had not lived there before the war, and could not speak with authority.

"*Sō, desu ne,*" my father agreed. "Completely."

There was a silence.

"*Ja...*" My father bowed and we turned to go, my father calling out the usual apologies. Leave-taking among Japanese can be interminable, but my father, being American, handled it efficiently.

Just before stepping out into the street, my father paused and called over his shoulder, "*Ne...* Around here...in the hills...wild mushrooms...still?"

The shop owner came out with us, scratching his head. "*Saaahh...*"

I heard him say, "I think so," among his murmured words, which sounded distinctly apologetic. In Japanese, tone is so much more important than content. The weak affirmation of his answer was more than negated by the surrounding vagueness. He couldn't bear to disappoint my father by saying no, there were no longer any wild mushrooms in the hills around Hiroshima.

The shop owner stood in front of his store bowing to us until we reached the corner and turned.

"Let's get something to eat," my father said, and later, as snowflakes began falling like a white rain covering the streets of Hiroshima, we sat in a noodle shop over steaming bowls of *tempura udon*, and he said, "So when are you coming home?"

DRIVING

TO COLMA

Through the glass pane I can see my sister Nancy. It's odd, the way they isolate you when you are coming from a foreign country — even if you are coming home. You cannot touch, you can't even speak, only exchange significant glances. On any other occasion we might have waved, or made faces. On any other occasion, my father would have been there to meet me. Now, however, Nancy turns away as soon as our eyes meet. I wonder if she is crying, as I pass down the stairs beneath the glassed-in gate area from which she has disappeared.

In the car, I wait for her to tell me.

"We have to concentrate," she says slowly, "on getting him to eat."

This is not what I am expecting. How long? I want to ask. How bad? Is he going to die? But she says nothing, and this is when I realize that they don't know. We will have to feel our way through each day without the reassurance of knowing our destination.

Nancy tells me that he has lost forty pounds in the past five weeks. The smell of food nauseates him.

"It's the drugs," she says. "The drugs do that to you."

All the rest of the way home I try to imagine my father, always a large, active and robust man, forty pounds lighter and refusing to eat. I think about the ten days in the hospital and the preceding months of pain when the doctor insisted it was arthritis and prescribed Tylenol with codeine. Still, when my mother embraces me at the door and leads me into the living room, I am not prepared for the shrunken, frail form sitting on the sofa.

"Gracie," he says.

I cross the room and bury my face in his neck; and I feel

at peace for the first time since Nancy's phone call three days before, telling me that I should probably come home.

"How was the flight back?" my mother asks.

"Fine. I slept the whole way. I had a beer, just to make sure."

Everyone laughs. The prodigal daughter has come home. We are all together, and everything will be all right.

In the following week, the focus of my life shrinks. All we can think about is: Will he eat? and then: What? My mother and I dig into the past for every old favorite we can remember. We count off calories and grams of protein, and make it through another day. My father has discovered a taste for lemonade. The exaggerated sweetness of it breaks through the drug-deadened tongue. We make it by the half-gallon.

There are also his pills. It is as though we have entered a new world and must learn the language spoken there. We list the strange vocabulary on a chart, with little boxes to be checked off for each pill taken, so many times a day. There seems to be an inexhaustible supply of allopurinol. This gives me hope. He will have to live a long time to finish all of those. Prednisone, four a day. Vitamins. There will be more names later: bleomycin, Oncovin, Decadron. Methotrexate and leucovorin. The names are strange, Russian-sounding. I roll the words around on my tongue. I suspect I will never forget them. I can fill my mind with recipes and names of drugs, and distract myself from the question that no one can answer.

I collect books, and curl up in my favorite reading place halfway up the stairs. Except now, instead of horse stories or mysteries, instead of Russian novels, they are medical books, dictionaries of my new language. I look up the

word: lymphoma. I look up allopurinol, prednisone, bleomycin, Oncovin, Decadron. Methotrexate is poison; leucovorin, the antidote. I repeat names, effects, and side
effects, like a child learning the Lord's Prayer, or a new
kind of catechism. I was always good in school.

At night, when I dream, I find myself back in my old
Japanese house. The sliding wood-framed windows are
opened wide to the trees outside, and the sun is on the tatami. I am sitting on the window ledge, waiting for Matsumoto to come through the gate, up the stone steps,
through the trees. But when I awaken, the fog is blanking
out the small square of window in the room where I slept as
a child. I am back in the house where I grew up, in the life I
have spent my life trying to escape, not because I hated it,
but because it had simply become too small.

It is two weeks before Japan enters my waking thoughts. It
is a Saturday, and Nancy is over. We have managed to ma-
neuver enough applesauce, ice cream, and cottage cheese
past his nausea to keep him alive. Our minds cannot yet
fathom the shape of cancer, but malnutrition is something
we can grasp. It is something we can fight.

I am fighting it today with rice pudding. I remembered
he once said he liked it. I was surprised because we had
never eaten it at home; it was a memory from some other
part of his life. It was disturbing to me as a child that there
were parts of my father's life that did not include me. Now I
don't mind as much. If he likes rice pudding, I will try to
make it, even though I know it won't be the rice pudding he
remembers. In fact, I don't even know what rice pudding is
supposed to taste like. In the past two weeks I have often
wished that I had lived my life differently, learned to cook,

for instance. I wonder if my father wishes it too. Wishes I had given him grandchildren, perhaps. Stayed around. I have spent too many of the last years of his life living in foreign countries. Immediately I censor the word "last."

We all stand around watching as he lifts the spoon to his mouth.

"How is it?" I ask.

Since my father became ill, I have realized how considerate of our feelings he always was. Illness makes a person self-centered, preoccupied with the immediacy of physical pain. Now, after one taste of my rice pudding, he puts the spoon down and pushes the bowl away. However, I am not devastated; I would probably not have eaten it either, especially with three pairs of eyes anxiously watching.

"Tokyo Stop," he says suddenly. "They have a pretty good *ten-don*."

Nancy heads into the dining room for her purse. "It's on twenty-fifth, isn't it?"

My mother is pulling a twenty from her purse.

"Somewhere around there," she says. "Get one for everybody."

There is nothing in my purse but Japanese yen from my other life, but out of habit I run and get it anyway. I get into the car with Nancy, blessing the marriage of East and West that has spawned Japanese fast food, and wonder what Tokyo Stop has besides *tempura donburi*.

The warmth of the day disorients me. Only two weeks ago it was winter in Japan. Unexpected snowfall in my coastal town had caught the plum blossoms on the castle grounds by surprise. I wonder when my boxes will arrive, containing the hastily packed pieces of my adult life. What they will not contain is snow-covered plum blossoms, sunlight on tatami, a woman sitting on a window ledge, waiting; all the things I can never explain when Nancy asks me, "So what was it you liked so much about Japan?" I noticed things more there; I was more alive. How can I explain that? And now I am home again, my other life like a phantom limb, gone, but so remembered that I can actually feel pain. I will call an old school friend, take in a movie. A funny, funny movie. Anything, to get started again.

For a while — days, perhaps — his appetite returns and he gets stronger. We tell ourselves it's over, a bad dream; he will be well by summer. Then the back pain returns. His only relief is when I massage him, digging my knuckles into the hollows on either side of his spine. I am frightened by how much bone I can feel. He lies on his side, moaning a strange, animal sound, and I kneel next to him, digging, making slow circles with my fists until my arms burn and go numb. His next treatment is three days away.

My father's specialist is located in the city. I will have to drive him there. I hate to drive — have not driven in years. I have never owned a car. I always walked, or took the bus. In Japan, I took the train.

I don't know why I dread driving so much. I was a fast learner, and got my license easily, but somewhere along the way I lost my confidence. I am especially terrified of driving on the freeway.

Before I go anywhere, I have to look at a map. I find my destination on it, then study the streets leading to it. I memorize which direction I will have to turn and when. When I go to a new place, I like to have the directions jotted on a piece of paper next to me, with the names of freeway exits; if possible, I would like to know which lane to be in, how many blocks before each turn.

Fortunately, Dr. Rothman's office is a straight shot down Geary Boulevard. I will not have to take the freeway at all.

It is strange to see my father's car cold and still in the garage. It is a luxury car, almost new. My father has never had a car for more than five years. He drives on business all over northern California. A good car is necessary. It seems he has always driven me wherever I had to go — to piano lessons, to school dances, to the airport. My father was always in the driver's seat. Now I'm the one holding the keys.

It is strange to be driving, with my father sitting on the passenger side. After a few jolting stops, he says, "You hit the brakes too late. You gotta start braking sooner."

"I'm not used to power brakes," I say, gripping the wheel to keep the anger out of my voice. For a moment I forget that my father is ill. He is just my father, telling me how to live my life. Silently I scream at him to shut up, to drive it himself if he doesn't like the way I drive, that I never wanted to be here driving this car. That I didn't want to be here at all. A moment later, I am glad I have not spoken aloud. Then I laugh to myself, remembering that my father used to make me put five cents into a can every time I said "shut up," usually to Nancy. I did not dare say it to him. Nancy was older, so if she said it, she had to pay a dime. It was important to my father that we act like ladies. I guess it didn't work. Or maybe it has.

Nancy has taken a few hours off from work and meets us at the doctor's office, dressed for success. She is a manager and likes her job. In fact, sometimes I sense that she wishes family relationships were more like work relationships. She knows how to handle employees. You can fire them if they don't shape up.

Today she is pressuring the receptionist in her best managerial manner. It is ten minutes past my father's appointment time. I sympathize with the receptionist, and am embarrassed.

Nancy approves of the nurse, who is cheerful and efficient as she measures out the various chemicals which will mingle with my father's blood and save or destroy him. The doctor pushes an IV needle into my father's arm and blood travels up the slender tubing. Then he shoots the chemicals, one by one, until the little bottles are all empty.

"It feels cold," my father says.

We ask the doctor about the future.

"The protocol," he says, "is six to ten treatments."

Protocol. I thought that meant how you were supposed to behave at a diplomatic gathering. But then, we are being diplomatic; we observe the ceremonies and courtesies expected of us and don't broach the burning questions.

"After all the tumor is destroyed," he explains, "we generally do a few more treatments for insurance."

"How many treatments does it take to destroy the tumor?" Nancy asks.

"That's a question I can't answer now," he says. "We'll just have to monitor the progress. But the protocol is six. Some cases require less, some more. We'll do a CAT scan at some point, to see how we're getting along."

"What point?" Nancy persists.

Dr. Rothman is patient. "It depends on how your father's recovery is progressing. Possibly after the sixth treatment."

I like Dr. Rothman. He has quiet gray eyes that really look at me. If he is hiding something from us, I feel quite sure that it is something we are better off not knowing. He speaks slowly, as if he wants us to hear what he is not saying as much as what he is saying. He is very gentle with my father, but knows how to tease him, too, and he seems to know just how much truth we can take.

Now he is looking directly at my father.

"So after approximately six treatments," he says, "we'll do another CAT scan; and if the tumor is gone, we generally do up to four more, just to make sure."

If the tumor is gone. The unstated condition is not lost on us. Even Nancy is silent, and suddenly, despite her tailored suit, her aggressive stance, she looks as lost, as powerless, as the rest of us.

In the evening my father begins to shake and sweat. As he lies shivering in bed, Nancy goes to him.

"He wants us to put in an automatic garage door opener," she reports.

"A what?" It is not the sort of last request I had been envisioning.

"An automatic garage door opener," she says. "He said it might be harder for him to lift the garage door by himself from now on. He wants to be able to get his car out."

In the morning the back pains are gone.

"I think I'll give Jim a call," he says.

Jim is an old fishing buddy. From the next room I can hear the anticipation in my father's voice as he asks to speak to Jim. He sounds like someone who has returned from a long trip and is anxious to tell someone that he's back.

"Well," he is saying, "I was kinda sick."

In the pause that follows I can almost hear Jim's concerned inquiry, and I brace myself for the answer.

"I have cancer," my father replies, glad to tell.

I find myself sympathizing with Jim, wondering how he will manage to respond to that.

"So how's fishing?" my father continues.

After hanging up, he comes into the dining room where I sit reading the paper.

"Jim's coming to visit," he says, looking as pleased as if he had landed a shark.

Jim comes, bringing half of a striped bass he caught out at Pacifica. I show him into the living room, tell him to sit down. He walks carefully, as if he is afraid of getting mud on our carpet even though he is not wearing his fishing boots. Jim has never been in our living room before; when he goes fishing with my dad, they come in and out through the garage. At first he refuses to sit; finally, he perches tentatively on a footstool. I leave them and go to the kitchen to make tea.

This is called *o-mimai*, I learn from my mother. It is the custom of calling on a friend to inquire about his health. The best part about it is that Japanese people bring wonderful things to eat when they come calling. Homemade sushi. Häagen-Dazs ice cream. Pastries from Japantown bakeries. My father and I hope that the Yamamuras will visit. Mrs. Yamamura makes a mean California roll.

In the next few days my father is bursting with energy. He goes out to water the back yard. He laughs and jokes like he used to, and formulates a plan to go back to work. He will drop by the office on a Friday, when all the other sales reps are there doing paperwork, and surprise them. I will drive him (at this, I picture the downtown location of his office, all the one-way streets and double-parked cars), and we'll stop and pick up three dozen donuts on the way. He looks forward to this. It is his next goal.

That weekend we have an automatic garage door opener installed, and my father cannot wait to try it out. He takes my mother for a short spin. A few minutes after they leave, the doorbell rings. It is Mr. Tanaka, a friend of the family, coming for *o-mimai*. He speaks in the hushed tones that people use when they speak of cancer.

"I was really shocked to hear about your father," he says. He sounds as though he is in church. I restrain a giggle. "How is he doing? Can he see visitors?"

"I'm afraid he's out right now," I say. Mr. Tanaka looks so startled that I start to giggle. "But he should be back in a few minutes. Won't you come in?" I gasp.

Mr. Tanaka murmurs his apologies and hands me the goodies. I thank him profusely, urging him to stay and wait.

"Really," I call to his departing back, "he ought to be back any minute now. I think he just went out to the beach."

Later, when I describe the look on Mr. Tanaka's face to my mother and father, we laugh until it seems there are no hospitals, no cancer, no death.

I have been home for almost a month, and now that my father is feeling better I am starting to panic about the fact that I have no job and no future. A month ago I had an office overlooking the Imperial Palace in Tokyo. I had friends, plans. And yet how sure I was when I picked up the phone and told my boss that I had to quit, had to go home. It was so clear that I was doing the right thing. Now I am wondering.

I start thinking about resumés and job application letters; but then I decide that I have to paint the sun room first.

The sun room has become a sort of warehouse, a museum filled with artifacts of our childhood. Long ago my sister and I played there during the summer. I decide that I will renovate it and claim it as my retreat. My mother is the curator of the museum, and against renovation.

"There's no heat," she says. "Why don't you move into Nancy's old room?"

I tell her that I had no central heating in Japan, and I liked it that way. The sun room is the nicest room in the house, the only room with windows on two sides and a view of the Pacific Ocean. I will move the artifacts of our childhood into my old bedroom and paint the sun room walls white. Then I will put my desk by the window overlooking the ocean, hang my watercolors of my Japanese house on the wall, and put my favorite books on a shelf.

"I'll get you a carpet for it," Nancy says.

"No thank you," I say. "I like the wood floor."

They think I am *enryo*-ing — declining out of politeness.

"What color do you want?" Nancy asks.

"I don't want any color," I say. "I don't want a carpet."

Nancy is startled by the anger in my voice.

"It'll be cold," my mother says.

My father comes in to see how the painting is going. He helps me run an extension cord into the room. My mother comes in once and bangs her leg on a dresser that I have moved.

"Everything's in a different place," she says.

After my office is set up, I spend hours there, writing letters, listening to Mozart, staring out the window at the ocean. There is no carpet, no heat, and I do as I please. My father sometimes comes in to visit. I move a chair into the warm sun for him. He likes the view of the ocean, admires the watercolors I have done of my Japanese house. We talk about summer in Japan — shaved ice, the sound of cicadas, fireworks by the river. He has never talked to us of these things before; before, I would not have understood. We hang out in my sun room like a couple of displaced persons congregating in a sanctuary, pursued by memories of our phantom other lives.

Five days after his treatment, my father goes off prednisone. Suddenly his energy is gone. He tires easily. Worst of all, he becomes depressed. His hair is beginning to fall out from the chemotherapy. He sits in silence, pulling out clumps of hair in disgust.

Ten days after the treatment my father is very weak. He develops mouth sores and cannot eat. His legs hurt.

His white cell count is low, Dr. Rothman says on the telephone. Restrict visitors; peel his fruit.

There is a brief respite before the back pain returns; and then it is time for number three.

The pattern becomes a clock by which we set our lives. By this time, I am working at night, teaching English to immigrants and refugees in a neighborhood church. They sit in a shell-shocked stupor, and sometimes the church seems like a bomb shelter where we have all gathered to escape the devastation of our individual worlds.

By this time we can predict when my father will be feeling well, so we can plan when to pick up the donuts and visit his office, when to make an appointment to get his car serviced. The dealer is down in Colma.

Nancy brings his car in, but by the time it is ready to be picked up, I have faced reality and bought a used car, and my father wants me to drive him down to pick up his car. Colma is a few miles south of San Francisco. I will have to take the freeway. I have been to Colma many times, but my father always drove. It's where all the cemeteries are.

"What's the best way to go?" I ask my father, getting out a map.

He has driven there a million times, but when it comes to explaining how to do it, he is at a loss.

"Just go down 19th Avenue," he says. "That's the easiest."

"And then what?"

"I'll tell you when we get there," he says.

My mother comes along for moral support. As we drive down 19th Avenue, with its bland, uniform houses facing each other across six lanes of traffic, its cold expanses of concrete occasionally adorned by an overcoated figure huddled against the chill of the fog, waiting for a bus, I remember dreary Saturday mornings when I was a child, growing up in this city. My mother and father and I would go grocery shopping at Safeway. I remember the unpleasant chill of the frozen foods section, the sight of people numbly loading their carts with packaged meat, paper towels, and soft drinks as though they moved in their sleep.

Then I remember my dream. I dreamed that I passed Matsumoto in the parking lot of Safeway. He was walking toward me, a stern expression on his face — the one that could melt so abruptly into laughter; that slight hunch of the shoulders that made him seem not as tall as he was. His black hair was swept back and curled slightly at the collar, giving him a wild look. In that colorless Safeway landscape, the energy of his movement, the life in his eyes, was almost obscene. I froze. My family was waiting for me in the car. He brushed by me, did not see me. I was unable to call his name. I woke up and I was alone, and now I am driving through the fog down 19th Avenue, toward the cemetery.

Before I know it, 19th becomes 280. My grip tightens on the steering wheel, and I ease up to fifty miles an hour.

"Now what?" I ask my father.

From the freeway I can see the gravestones on the hillside.

"Get over to the right," he says. "Take the next exit."

My father guides me through a series of turns, and in a few minutes we are pulling into the Buick dealer's lot. My grip loosens on the steering wheel. Going back should be easier; all I have to do is reverse the process, and, besides, I will be able to follow my father's car.

His car is not quite ready. We have to wait a half an hour. The waiting seems to tire him. We should have started out earlier in the day; it is getting on to late afternoon. Finally the car is ready to go.

As we are about to start back, my mother gets into the car with me. This surprises me, as I assumed she would ride with my father. My mother has always gone with my father, has always been at his side. Perhaps she feels that I am in greater need of moral support. Or perhaps she is simply preparing; she will have to get used to riding with me from now on.

I follow my father back onto the freeway. Traffic is light,

so it's easy to stay behind him. I can see his head, the cap that he is wearing to cover his baldness. My father is a handsome man; he was always proud of his full head of hair. His head looks smaller without the hair. Suddenly he seems terribly vulnerable. If anything happens, he is all alone. We will be unable to help him.

He begins moving to the right. I follow. He is signaling to let me know that he's going to exit. The sign says "Pacifica."

"Where's he going?" I ask my mother, panicking. Pacifica is in the opposite direction from home.

I follow him onto the Pacifica exit. We loop around and start heading south.

"What's he doing?" Home is north.

I feel utterly helpless. There is no way to communicate with him, ask him what he is doing, thinking. Stop, I want to shout. We need to talk.

His right-turn signal begins flashing. I am exasperated. How like him. This is the way it's always been. All my life, my father has never explained himself, never communicated except through cryptic signals, while the rest of us puzzled over them and inevitably followed. I follow him off the freeway, onto an unfamiliar street.

He winds around and gets back onto the freeway, going in the opposite direction.

"This is really too much," I say to my mother, completely unnerved. "What the hell . . ."

Another exit and loop, and we are back on 280 north, where we started.

It occurs to me that he had taken a wrong turn. Taking the Pacifica exit had been a mistake — that was all. I feel great relief at the logical explanation.

Just as I begin to relax, we approach the Pacifica exit, and again he signals to exit.

"He's doing the same thing!" I explode.

Until now I have never considered the possibility that the drugs were affecting my father's mind. Suddenly I wonder if he is confused, if he is in control of his actions. I am terrified. He is all alone in a separate car and there is nothing I can do for him.

For a wild moment I consider staying on 280 and getting my mother safely home, at least. But if my father is in trouble, I cannot abandon him. I signal and follow him toward Pacifica.

We loop over 280 and descend southward once again, but this time my father moves immediately right and takes an exit I did not see the first time. It says "Skyline." There is another branch, one going south, the other north. My father heads north, between rolling hills that lead to the sea.

Then, abruptly, the landscape flattens out just as we go over a rise, and off in the distance I can see the ocean, the unbroken line of the horizon, lit for sunset, leading us homeward. So this is what he was trying to do. He wanted to see this.

For an instant, we hover at the top of the rise, as if in greeting, as if in parting. Then we hurry toward the falling darkness.

SEATTLE

Every time I go over to my mother's house, she tells me about the Japanese program that was on TV last week. She usually sits across the breakfast room table from me as I am trying to read the paper, and begins by asking, "Did you see the Japanese program last Saturday night?"

My answer is always "No," but she always asks me anyway. I continue to read, hoping that my concentration on the news will put an end to the topic; however, she always persists.

"It was good," she says, and when I don't respond, she adds, "You would've liked it."

I turn a page.

She watches more TV now, ever since my father died. When he was alive, she always said she was too busy. Too much to do around the house; no time to just sit around. Now that he is gone, I have sometimes dropped in unexpectedly and found her in front of the television in the middle of the afternoon. The Japanese program is her favorite. There are endless historical dramas, modern-day soap operas, and one-hour family dramas about wandering husbands or nasty mothers-in-law. My mother is especially fond of the mother-daughter stories.

"There was this mother and daughter," she begins, unperturbed by the fact that I am still buried in my newspaper. "The father died . . . " And she tells me, in minute detail, the whole story.

I tried watching one once, to keep her company, but the pathos and self-sacrifice drove me from the room before it was even halfway through. I have nothing against pathos, but it has to be done well. I admit I have a harder time with self-sacrifice.

After my father died, at the funeral in fact, several people came up to me and said, "It would be nice if you moved in with your mother." I thought about it. I thought about her, who had never lived alone in her life, all by herself in that big house. In some ways it would be very convenient. She would want to cook for me, do my laundry. I could drive her to the supermarket, to doctors' appointments, to funerals. From the Japanese standpoint, it was the expected thing to do. A divorced daughter, over thirty — a mother, over sixty, left alone. I wavered.

But I am not Japanese. I tried to imagine what it would be like, if I moved back in with my mom. I tried to picture my furniture in the already furnished rooms of her house. Where would my bed go? My desk? I would have to pack away all my dishes again. I imagined going to work every day at the Consulate, and coming home to my mother's house. I tried to imagine inviting friends over — not childhood ones, but adult ones. Friends who drink, smoke. I tried to imagine making love to Yoshi on her couch.

Perhaps I've just seen too many American movies. In American movies getting everything you want constitutes a happy ending. A satisfying Japanese ending, in contrast, has to have an element of sadness. There must be suffering and sacrifice — for these are proof of love. I've always hated stories where everybody sacrifices themselves and nobody ends up happy. It is a compulsion that strikes me as a form of mental illness, and I don't want to hear about it, much less do it.

Today I have a story of my own to tell. I wonder how I will begin. "I may be going to Japan," I will say. She will be silent, knowing immediately in that way mothers have that I don't mean on vacation. No — I can't begin that way. Maybe I should just come right out and say, "Miyagawa-san has asked me to marry him." But then she will say, "Isn't he already married?" And I will say, "He is going to leave his wife." And then we will fight. No, I will have to tell it from the inside out, so that it doesn't sound like a made-for-television movie. I will have to give her more warning. Something gradual but ominous, like, "Let's sit down. I need to have a talk with you."

I find her in the living room, watching the news.

"Hi, Mom."

"Hi," she says, getting up. She switches the television off. "How are you?"

"Okay." I head down to the basement with my laundry. I always bring my laundry to my mother's house. It gives me something to do while I'm there. I duck under the clothesline, noting that it seems to have dropped another couple of inches since the last time I was there. I am a head taller than my mother, and my father was taller than me. When he was alive, there were no low-hanging clotheslines.

When I come back upstairs, my mother is sitting at the dining room table, waiting. I go into the kitchen, pour myself some orange juice. Then I sit down at the breakfast room table and open the paper.

She comes over and sits across from me.

"Guess who I ran into the other day?" she begins.

"Who?"

"Rhonda, Kenji's wife. Do you remember her? I was walking up Geary Street on my way back from the supermarket and she was coming the other way. I hadn't seen her in years, but I recognized her right away. She recognized me, too."

When I was about ten, Kenji and my dad had worked together, selling for an importing company. I remembered Kenji as a pleasant, conscientious young man with a nice smile. His wife, Rhonda, was young and pretty but rather aloof.

"How is she?" I ask, checking my horoscope to see what the week has in store for me.

"She seemed really happy to see me," my mother says. "We stood on the street talking for almost a half hour."

"Oh?"

"She was telling me all her troubles."

"Mhmm . . ."

"She and Kenji are separated. Apparently he has a girlfriend in Seattle, someone he met and used to visit on his business trips. Rhonda found out about it and kicked him out of the house. The kids won't speak to him."

I stop reading.

"The Japanese program always has stories like that," my mother continues. "The husband is sent away to some other city on business, and he falls in love with another woman. I guess men are just weak."

I have sometimes wondered if my mother is psychic. Is she being incredibly subtle, indirect, and Japanese — or am I being paranoid? I search her face for a clue. Did she really run into this Rhonda, or is she making it all up? How could she possibly know about Yoshi and me? I am certain that I have done no more than mention his name, among many other names of interesting people I meet through my job at the Consulate. I have never let on about the drinks after work, the dinners — the weekends away. And I have barely acknowledged, even to myself, the family back in Japan.

"Although I have to say," she continues, "that I always liked Kenji. He was a very nice person. When Daddy was in Japan on business once Kenji came over and told me to call him if I needed anything. Not everyone would do that. He was very thoughtful. I can understand how some woman might misinterpret that."

"Maybe she wasn't misinterpreting anything," I say. "Maybe he wasn't happy with Rhonda. Maybe she was cold. Maybe he found something with that woman in Seattle that Rhonda couldn't give him."

"Maybe," my mother says. But she is only filling an uncomfortable silence.

"There must be some nice girls up in Seattle," she continues. "Daddy used to sell to an old *issei* couple up there that had some nice daughters; I remember him telling me. They invited him to dinner once, and he even went mushroom-picking with them. Three daughters, I think there were." And then she is silent; and I can think of nothing to say.

I had wanted to tell my mother that I had been determined not to fall in love with Yoshi, but it happened anyway. It didn't start out being about love at all. It was his openness, his curiosity, that made me want to share with him everything I liked best about America. And then I discovered his playfulness, his capacity for happiness. We spent much of our time together chattering and laughing like two children. That's when it happened. I wanted to tell my mother what Yoshi had told me the day he left for Japan. He had come hurrying up my steps with two bunches of flowers in a paper bag. He said he had enjoyed living, since he met me. He did not want to hurt his children, but he wanted to start over before it was too late. Would I marry him, if he left his wife?

I had wanted to tell my mother all this, but instead, I go over and put my arms around her shoulders and I say, "You were lucky, Mom. Daddy wasn't like that."

Maybe I will tell her my story the next time I come. Or perhaps she will have one to tell me, another mother-daughter tale from the Japanese program. It is always the same story. There are minor variations. Sometimes the mother is very old-fashioned, sometimes modern, even outrageous. But underneath it all she always has the same Japanese heart. Sometimes the daughter marries and leaves, sometimes it's the mother who marries, unexpect-edly, or fabricates a fictitious marriage proposal so that the daughter will not feel obligated to stick around. What is al-ways the same is the invisible wires that bind them, the bond of obligation, of suffering, of love — and this is why my mother likes these dramas; because this is the way she would like real life to be.

R.A. Sasaki is a third-generation San Franciscan. She attended the University of Kent in Canterbury, has a B.A. from the University of California at Berkeley, and an M.A. in Creative Writing from San Francisco State University. Winner of the 1983 American Japanese National Literary Award, she has had stories published in the *Short Story Review* and *Making Waves: An Anthology of Writing by Asian-American Women*. *The Loom and Other Stories* is her first published collection. She currently lives in Berkeley, California.

This book was designed by Tree Swenson.
It is set in Perpetua type by The Typeworks
and manufactured by Maple-Vail
on acid-free paper.

The cover art is a detail
from an Edo period screen
entitled "Weavers and Dyers,"
MOA Museum, Atami, Japan.

Author photo by Rob Leri.

SHORT FICTION / / / ISBN 1-55597-157-1 / / / $10.00

THE
L O O M
AND OTHER STORIES

R. A. SASAKI

The nine short stories in this collection combine into a moving portrait of three generations of Japanese-Americans trying to fit themselves into the fabric of American society. The author writes: "I wandered ghostlike amidst the mainstream of America, treading unaware on a culture that lay buried like a lost civilization beneath my feet, unaware of the cultural amnesia inflicted on my parents' generation by the internment and the atomic bomb."

Poignant, heart-breaking, and often funny, these tales chronicle the pains and hopes of family members reaching out in individual ways to understand themselves, their families, and their community.

"Ruth Sasaki writes with great self-knowledge, with a sensitivity born of examined experience, and with a wonderfully humorous insight of the American ethnic experience."
— GUS LEE, author of *China Boy*

THE GRAYWOLF SHORT FICTION SERIES

GRAYWOLF
PRESS

ISBN 1-55597-157-1

51000>

9 781555 971571